ALSO BY
STUART McLEAN

FICTION

Stories from the Vinyl Cafe

Home from the Vinyl Cafe

Vinyl Cafe Unplugged

Vinyl Cafe Diaries

Dave Cooks the Turkey

Secrets from the Vinyl Cafe

Extreme Vinyl Cafe

NON-FICTION

The Morningside World of Stuart McLean

Welcome Home: Travels in Smalltown Canada

Vinyl Cafe Notebooks

EDITED BY STUART McLEAN

When We Were Young:
An Anthology of Canadian Stories

To Alistair and Stephanie

STUART McLEAN

REVENGE of the VINYL CAFE

VIKING

VIKING
an imprint of Penguin Canada

Published by the Penguin Group
Penguin Group (Canada),
90 Eglinton Avenue East, Suite 700, Toronto, Ontario, Canada M4P 2Y3

Penguin Group (USA) Inc., 375 Hudson Street, New York, New York 10014, U.S.A.
Penguin Books Ltd, 80 Strand, London WC2R 0RL, England
Penguin Ireland, 25 St Stephen's Green, Dublin 2, Ireland (a division of Penguin Books Ltd)
Penguin Group (Australia), 250 Camberwell Road, Camberwell, Victoria 3124, Australia
(a division of Pearson Australia Group Pty Ltd)
Penguin Books India Pvt Ltd, 11 Community Centre, Panchsheel Park,
New Delhi – 110 017, India
Penguin Group (NZ), 67 Apollo Drive, Rosedale, Auckland 0632, New Zealand
(a division of Pearson New Zealand Ltd)
Penguin Books (South Africa) (Pty) Ltd, 24 Sturdee Avenue, Rosebank,
Johannesburg 2196, South Africa

Penguin Books Ltd, Registered Offices: 80 Strand, London WC2R 0RL, England

First published 2012

1 2 3 4 5 6 7 8 9 10 (RRD)

Manufactured in the U.S.A.

LIBRARY AND ARCHIVES CANADA CATALOGUING IN PUBLICATION

McLean, Stuart, 1948
Revenge of the vinyl cafe / Stuart McLean.

Short stories.
ISBN 978-0-670-06474-8

I. Title.

PS8575.L448R49 2012   C813'.54   C2012-904430-X

Visit *The Vinyl Cafe* website at **www.vinylcafe.com**

Visit the Penguin Canada website at **www.penguin.ca**

Special and corporate bulk purchase rates available; please see
www.penguin.ca/corporatesales or call 1-800-810-3104, ext. 2477.

ALWAYS LEARNING   PEARSON

HELLO, MONSTER

*I have something you should know. I have Monster Spray
here. If you try anything, I will use it.*
  —MAX, THE BOY

It was one of those moments that make you wonder if
your life is cursed. One of those moments when you start
to believe that the universe is not, in fact, a random place,
but an intelligent one, and that the universal intelligence is a
malevolent intelligence, or it is, at least, when it comes to you.

Dave was standing on the sidewalk, just down the street
from his friend Kenny Wong's café. In fact, he had been *in*
Kenny's for the last hour or so. Now he was standing on the
corner, contemplating what he was going to do next.

His wife, Morley, and his son, Sam, were away for the
weekend, so there was no rush to get home. He had three
glorious days of solitude ahead of him.

He wondered if he should go over to the Lowbeers' and
check on their cat.

The Lowbeers were away too. Dave was feeding the
Lowbeers' cat for the weekend. Now that he thought of it, he
wasn't sure where he had put their keys—whether he had
them with him, that is, or whether he had left them at home.

And that is why he dug them out of his pocket; that is how
he came to be holding the Lowbeers' keys as he stood on the
corner down the street from Kenny's café.

Why he dropped them? Who knows. These sorts of things happen. That is the part about the world being cursed.

He pulled the keys out of his pocket and was standing there considering whether he should feed the cat now or later when they slipped out of his hand and fell towards the ground, in the slow-motiony way that disasters favour.

They hit the sidewalk and bounced into the gutter.

Later Dave would say that you could line up a thousand people and have them drop a thousand sets of keys and nothing more would happen.

He is probably right. Probably if you dropped a thousand sets of keys, not one other set would bounce into the gutter like the Lowbeers' did; and if they did, they would have lain there on top of the sewer grate.

These didn't. These *landed* on the sewer grate, balanced there for a moment, like a golf ball balancing on the lip of a golf hole, and then they slowly, unbelievably, and maybe even deliberately, disappeared.

Vanished.

Dave stared at where they had been in disbelief—at where they had been and weren't anymore.

"Seriously?" he said.

He got down on his hands and his knees and peered into the sewer. There was nothing but darkness down there.

He pulled at the sewer grate. It didn't budge.

If he hadn't been so close to his record store, that probably would have been the end to this. He would have tried to pull the sewer grate free, and he would have failed, and that would have been that.

CONTENTS

"Smith Gardner," said Margaret,
"life would be pretty tedious if all we did
was stick to the facts."

Unfortunately, he was able to walk back to his store in no time flat. Unfortunately, in no time flat, he was back at the sewer with a flashlight and a crowbar. Unfortunately, five minutes after he had dropped the Lowbeers' keys down the sewer, he had, with the help of the crowbar, jimmied the sewer cover off and was climbing down the cold steel rungs set into the vertical concrete wall.

Ten minutes after he had dropped the keys, Dave was standing at the bottom of the sewer holding them triumphantly in his hand.

He will never know, for certain, what happened next. But he knows this much for sure—he was standing down there, with the keys in his hand, feeling triumphant, when there was the cold and ominous clang of steel above him. Like a prison door slamming. And the dim sewer was suddenly dimmer.

His best guess is that a city truck came along, and a city worker spotted the grate he had removed and left lying in the gutter. Whatever transpired up there didn't matter. What mattered was that he was now trapped at the bottom of the sewer with the Lowbeers' keys, a flashlight and nothing else.

He scurried back up the ladder and pressed his face to the grate.

"Hey!" he called. "I'm *down* here."

And then a car rolled over the grate and stopped. Dead. A door opened and someone got out of the car. The door closed and whoever it was, walked away. A few seconds later the car's horn beeped to confirm the doors were locked.

"You've got to be kidding," said Dave.

It was awkward holding onto the ladder at the top the way he was. He climbed back down to the bottom. He was standing there now—his hand on the bottom rung of the ladder.

Let me be clear, this was a storm sewer he was standing in. Not a sewer-sewer. This was where the rainwater went. He was standing at the bottom of the ladder, looking along a concrete pipe, maybe five feet around. He played his flashlight down the tunnel. About fifty yards away, there was a faint pool of light. Another sewer grate, he suspected. Another ladder to freedom.

He bowed his head and splashed off towards the light.

In the next hour or so, Dave covered a mile, maybe more. He climbed a dozen or two ladders. He lost count. For the next hour or so, he lurched along the sewer and shoved his shoulder against grate after grate—but something that required a crowbar from above wasn't about to give in to a shoulder from below.

He kept going.

He had stumbled into an underground world that he knew existed but had never considered. If it hadn't been such an astonishing world, he might have been afraid.

From time to time, other pipes joined his like little tributaries. His flashlight bounced against the walls and along the little stream at his feet.

He came across a section where the walls were fashioned of red, water-stained brick. And soon after that, he stepped into an underground brick room with a vaulted twenty-foot ceiling. It was like stumbling upon the ruins of an abandoned church. He looked around the brick chamber in wonder. He could have been in the sewers of London.

And that, strangely, is the moment he had his first whiff of fear. In the beautiful underground brick room. Not coming into it. Coming into it, he had been swept away by its unexpected majesty. The fear came on his way out.

There were three pipes leaving the far end of the chamber. As he stared at them, wondering which he should take, he glanced back the way he had come. He played his flashlight against the far wall and saw that there were three pipes at the other end too. He had no idea which one he had emerged from. He realized, for the first time, he had no idea where he was— and more importantly, that he couldn't get back to where he had come from. He was lost.

That's when he felt fear.

Suddenly the sewer seemed darker. The ceiling seemed heavier, the walls closer. Everything was pressing in on him. His breath was becoming shallow and fast.

Nothing had changed, of course. He wasn't empirically lost. It was more like he had stepped into some parallel universe. He was in the underground. Connected to, yet apart from, the world he knew. It was as if he were a ghost.

He splashed along, but with more urgency now—and a gnawing, fluttery stomach.

It was an hour later that he met the boy.

By then he had been down there maybe three hours, wandering along the pipes, both narrow and wide, and through the unexpected rooms, going from ladder to ladder, climbing from grate to grate, calling out—at first into streets with too much traffic for anyone to hear him, and then later, into some preternaturally quiet corner of the city that didn't even seem to have pedestrians.

The boy caught him completely by surprise.

He had climbed up yet another ladder, pressed his face against yet another grate, and called out as he had called out before.

"Hello? Helloo-*oo*."

Like all the other times, there was no reply, no acknowledgement of his existence.

"Hello. Is anyone there?"

He was halfway back down the ladder when a tiny voice said, "*I'm* here."

Dave, not quite believing he had heard that, wondering if he had *imagined* that, scrambled back to the top rung.

"What?" he asked. "What did you say?"

"I said, '*I'm* here.'"

Dave pressed his face against the grate and let go of the ladder with one hand so he could lean out and twist around. No matter which way he twisted, all he could see ... was sky.

Before he could say anything else, the boy spoke.

The boy said, "Are you ... a monster? Are you a monster who has come to get me?"

Dave laughed.

"No," he said, "I am not a monster. I'm trapped in the sewer. Where are we?"

The boy said, "At my place. We're at my place. If you are not a monster, what are you doing in the sewer?"

"Good question," said Dave.

"I know," said the boy.

There was a longish pause while they both considered this.

Dave said, "Are you still there?"

The boy said, "Maybe."

Dave said, "You don't have to be afraid. There *aren't* actually monsters, you know."

And the boy said, "That's what my mother says. My mother says there are no monsters under my bed, and no monsters in my cupboard, and no monsters behind the shower curtain."

"Is your mother home?" asked Dave.

"I can't tell you that," said the boy. "My cousin says the monsters live in the sewer.

"If you are not a monster, are you a Wild Thing? Are you a Wild Thing who has come to take me away in a boat? Is there going to be a rumpus?"

"No," said Dave. "I am not a Wild Thing."

"That's too bad," said the boy.

Dave said, "I need your help. I am trapped down here. I got trapped by accident. Can you go and tell your mother there is someone in the sewer?"

"No," said the boy.

"Why not?" asked Dave.

"Because I would get in trouble for talking to a stranger," said the boy.

Dave said, "I am not a monster. And I am not a Wild Thing. I'm not a stranger. Just get your mother. You won't get in trouble."

"You don't know my mother," said the boy.

Dave pushed up against the grate. It didn't budge.

If he leaned way out to the left, he could see the boy's shoes. And his legs up to his knees. The boy was wearing sneakers and jeans. The jeans were rolled at the bottom. He was sitting on the sidewalk, his feet in the gutter.

"Have you seen Vanessa?" asked the boy.

"What?" said Dave.

The boy said Vanessa was his goldfish. One morning last week, the boy had found Vanessa lying at the bottom of her bowl—on her side.

While he was at school, his mother had taken Vanessa to the vet, and the vet had to keep her in a special tank, but she was happy and had lots of friends. She just couldn't come home. Ever.

"Why would *I* see her?" asked Dave.

"Because my cousin said Vanessa didn't go to the vet at all. My cousin said he saw my mother flush Vanessa down the toilet.

"Where do goldfish go when they die?"

"Sometimes into special tanks at the vets," said Dave. "Sometimes down the toilet."

"That's what I thought," said the boy. "Are *you* dead?"

"Not yet," said Dave.

Maybe they talked for fifteen minutes. Maybe it was an hour. It was hard to tell. Dave had lost his sense of time.

They talked for a while, anyway, and then the boy said, "I have to go now."

"What?" said Dave, "Wait a minute!"

And the boy said, "I can't. It's suppertime."

And he stood up.

And Dave said, "Wait!"

There was no answer. The boy had gone.

Dave shoved his face right up against the sewer grate.

"Hey," he shouted. "I have your goldfish!"

A night in a sewer is not a happy thing. A night in a sewer is dark and damp. And you are alone. And as the night goes on, you start hearing things. Scurrying things.

Occasionally, but not often, a car goes by above you, and you see the flash of the headlights. But mostly, it is dark. You fall asleep, but you keep waking up. And when you do, you have no idea if you have been asleep for a long time or a short time. Or maybe you haven't been asleep at all. All you know for sure is that it is dark. So dark you can't see your hand when you hold it right in front of your face. And you are hungry. Probably as hungry as the Lowbeers' cat.

So there is guilt too. But mostly there is fear, and as the night deepens, desperation.

"Hello, monster?"

Dave had fallen asleep again. He was sitting at the bottom of the ladder. His head was on his chest.

"Monster? Are you there?"

It was still pitch-dark.

Dave scrambled up the ladder. He could see stars and the glow from a distant street lamp, but he couldn't see anything else.

"I brought you something to eat," said the boy.

The boy was pushing a narrow cellophane-wrapped package through the sewer grate.

Dave reached out to take it. The boy let go and jerked his hand back.

Whatever it was fell. When it reached the bottom, there was a splash.

And that's when Dave, overcome with desperation, thought if he could just get the boy a bit closer, he might be able to thrust his hand through the grate and grab him. The boy would scream for help, of course. But someone would hear him screaming, and they would come. His parents would come. And Dave would be saved. It is a testament to the power of solitary confinement to dull a person's mind that Dave thought this might be a *good* idea.

"Want to see something?" asked Dave.

"You can't trick me," said the boy.

The boy stood up. He was leaving.

"Wait," said Dave. "Promise you'll come back."

"After breakfast," said the boy.

It was Saturday morning. Dave had been in the sewer fourteen hours.

The boy was back.

He was kneeling on the sidewalk now. Dave couldn't see his face, but he could see his striped T-shirt. His skinny arms.

"Thank you for the sandwich," said Dave. "It was good."

"You're welcome," said the boy.

"I have to go to swimming," said the boy.

And then ever so slowly, his little hand came through the sewer grate again. He was holding something. It was a tiny yellow dump truck. Dave reached out.

When Dave's fingers folded around the small toy, the boy jerked his hand away.

Dave held the truck in his hand.

"You can play with that until I come back," said the boy.

Dave put the truck in his pocket and his fingers through the top of the grate.

"That was very brave," said Dave.

"Yes," said the boy. "I know."

The boy reached out, ever so tentatively, and touched Dave's finger, jerking his hand back again almost immediately.

"Are you still scared?" asked Dave.

"Yes," said the boy.

Then he said, "I have to go now."

"Wait," said Dave. "Do you *want* me to be a monster?"

"I am not sure," said the boy. "I can't decide."

And he ran away.

And now Dave was standing at the bottom of the ladder. He was starving. And tired. He was damp and dirty. He was itchy. He needed a shave.

Presumably, if he set off and followed the flow of the water in the sewer, it would lead him somewhere. Presumably, if he kept trying sewer grates along the way, someone would eventually hear him.

Or not. Possibly, if he started wandering around, he would just wander around in circles. Possibly no one would hear him at all.

He thought about heading off. He decided to stay.

He was waiting when the boy came back.

"I am not a monster, you know. I'm just a father. And I got stuck."

"That's what you say," said the boy.

The boy came back an hour later with a rope.

"I have decided to pull the lid off," said the boy.

He fed one end of the rope through the sewer cover. Dave tied it to the grate, like the boy told him to.

The boy tied the other end to his bicycle.

Then he knelt down on the grate and said, "I have something you should know. I have Monster Spray here. If you try anything, I will use it."

He held a plastic spray bottle up to the grate. The label was hand lettered. It said Monster Spray.

The boy got on his bike. The rope tightened.

"Now," said the boy.

Dave threw his shoulder against the grate.

"It didn't budge," said the boy.

"Nope," said Dave. "But it was a nice try. Where did you get the rope?"

"From my mother," said the boy

"What did you tell her you were doing with it?"

"Rescuing a monster from the sewer," said the boy.

An hour passed.

And then another.

Dave heard them before he saw them, their voices echoing along the pipe. Then a moment or two later, he saw the beams from their flashlights bouncing along the walls.

Two of them—an inspection team.

"Lookie, lookie," said the older guy, when they saw Dave.

"I dropped my keys," said Dave. "I got lost."

The younger one said, "You can come with us."

Dave said, "Can you wait a minute?"

He climbed up the ladder. He pressed his face against the grate. He called out one last time.

"Hello," he called "Are you there? I have to go. I'm sorry."

The boy brought his mother after supper.

"We have to be careful," said the boy. "You hold the spray."

"And what do I do with it?" asked the mother.

"If he tries anything funny—spray him," said the boy.

The boy knelt down.

"Get ready," he said.

Then he called out.

"Monster," he said. "Monster. Monster. Are you there?"

There was no answer.

The boy turned around and looked at his mother. She was holding the spray in front of her. She was ready.

"It's okay," said the boy. "He's gone."

The boy lay down on his belly and peered in.

The mother looked at her watch.

"Sweetie," said the mother, "you know monsters only exist in stories, don't you? There aren't any monsters under the bed. And there aren't any monsters in the sewer, and …"

But the boy wasn't listening. The boy was peering into the sewer. Now he was reaching into it, his skinny arm reaching down.

"Look," he said.

The mother knelt beside him, and then she lay down, and they peered together.

His yellow dump truck was balanced on the top rung of the ladder.

"He left me my truck," said the boy.

"I can't reach it," he said. "You get it."

The mother reached in and pulled it out for him. She held it up and frowned.

"How did that get there?" she asked.

"I told you," said the boy. "The monster."

He put the truck in his pocket. And they walked back to the house, holding hands. The boy, whose name is Max, and his mother, who twice looked over her shoulder and back at the sewer before they went inside.

ANNIE'S TURN

It's definitely not a log. I saw it move. I think it's a wolf.
—BILLY

In those days, they would always set something onto the ice out on the lake in front of the Breakwater Hotel. An old car, an outhouse, a rusted-out tractor—some old rig. They would set it there on New Year's Day and then take bets about when it was going to disappear.

That winter, it was Stumpy Hayman's woodshed. And on a weekend, early that spring, Pete Levine and Charlie Fraser, who both had money riding on it, tried to get out there to give the doomed woodshed a hand. The woodshed was just about through anyway, the ice all slushy and rotten, and all the fishing huts back on land. Heck, you could see open water out in the middle.

Pete and Charlie almost went through the ice themselves and had to retreat. Pete, who was swearing like a sailor when they were back on shore, stumbled into the hotel dining room, soaked.

Now, this was a long time ago. They don't do this anymore. People are sensitive to putting that sort of stuff into the lake these days.

This was the winter Dave was just twelve, just tall enough that if he stood on his bedroom radiator, held on to the window frame and leaned way out to the left, he could make out the woodshed roof over the treetops and rooftops of the town.

"Is it still there?" asked Charlie, Dave's dad, who was bouncing up and down in the hallway.

Charlie had bet on a Sunday two weeks out. And Charlie was convinced that if the woodshed could hold on through the weekend, the weather was going to take a turn for the worse and give him a shot at the pot.

"A *good* shot," said Charlie.

It *was* possible.

They were balanced in that precarious no man's land between the seasons. It was neither spring nor winter. It *could* have gone either way. There was still snow all about— pushed up at the end of the driveway and piled along the road—but it was spring snow. All granular and icy, like corn kernels. Every morning, Old Man Macaulay would get up and stare wistfully at his maple bush. Any day, things were going to start stirring.

The next Thursday, the woodshed was still out there. "I'm telling you," said Charlie at breakfast as he reached for the honey, "I'm just telling you."

Charlie had promised everyone in the family a share if he won.

"Five dollars," he said.

"Each?" said Dave.

"Each," said Charlie.

"Me too?" said Annie.

Annie, who was not yet ten that winter, didn't have confidence that she would necessarily be included.

"You too," said Charlie.

Annie nodded earnestly.

"Me too," she said to Dave.

So every morning at breakfast, Dave, who could see the lake from his bedroom window, reported in.

And it was that Thursday, the week after Pete and Charlie had almost drowned, when Dave climbed up to have a look just before supper that he saw the wolf.

Although he didn't know it was a wolf then.

At first it didn't look like anything. At first he thought it was just a shadow, a smudge of darkness on the snow.

"Dave. It's dinner."

If you looked carefully, it seemed to be *something*. He turned off his bedroom light and tried again. Squinting. It was hard to tell if someone had *left* something out there maybe, or if maybe it was a log poking through the ice.

Or even just his imagination. Your eyes could play tricks on you at dusk, the line between land and sky blurred, not to mention between wolf and log.

"*Dave!* Supper."

It was Billy Mitchell who said *wolf*.

Billy, who lived in town and could see out across the water perfectly.

Dave phoned Billy after supper and Billy said, "It's definitely not a log. I saw it move. I think it's a wolf."

"A wolf," said Dave.

"I can *see* it clearly," said Billy, "its yellow fangs."

Of course they went and checked it out—Dave, Billy, and Chan Gillespie, on Friday, as soon as school was out. Hustling down River Street, past Rutledge's Hardware and MacDonnell's General Store, then around Kerrigan's to the town dock. From the dock, they followed the little path at the back of the parking lot down to the beach—as empty as a pocket at that time of year.

At first they didn't see it. They got to the beach and—

"It's gone," said Billy.

But it wasn't gone.

"There," said Dave.

It was further out than it had been the night before.

"It's just a log," said Chan, who had brought a knife in case it wasn't.

Billy lobbed a snowball.

And the log jumped up and started barking.

"A dog," said Dave.

It was on a big hunk of ice. The ice was surrounded by water. It was on an ice island.

They called to it. "Come here," Dave said. "Come on. Come here."

The dog dropped down on its front paws and held its rear high, its tail wagging. Then it took maybe three steps sideways and then four towards them, but it sunk into the slush on the edge of the ice, scrambled back and stood there barking.

"What's the matter with it?" asked Billy.

"He can't swim," said Dave.

"How do *you* know?" said Billy.

"You can tell," said Dave, "by the fact that he is not swimming."

Billy went and got a rope.

Dave and Chan went to Kerrigan's and got a big beef bone from the butcher.

They tied the bone to the rope.

Billy threw it.

It landed, with a splash, in the water. Short. Billy tried again and then again. They each tried. But no one got any closer. And the dog wasn't budging.

Dave said, "We need a boat."

Chan went home and got his toboggan instead.

The tied the rope around Dave's waist.

"That way," said Chan, "if you fall through the ice, they won't have to drag for your body."

And Dave set off, pulling the toboggan behind him like an arctic explorer. When he got to the edge of the water, he put the toboggan down and gave it a shove.

The toboggan was supposed to float out to the ice island, the dog was supposed to climb onto it, then Dave was supposed to pull him back, across the open water. They had tied the soup bone to the front of the toboggan to entice the dog.

But when the toboggan hit the water, it sank like a stone.

It was getting dark.

"I have to go," said Billy.

"I have to go too," said Chan.

Dave stood on the edge of the shore and shouted at the dog. "We'll be back. Tomorrow. Stay."

That night as the boys slept, spring finally made up its mind and snuck softly into town. It came on the wings of crows. Everyone woke to the cawing. It was as if winter had never been.

"It is beautiful," said Margaret as she stood on the front stoop.

The yard was suddenly soft, the road muddy and wet.

"You can feel the sun," said Charlie, putting his arm around his wife. "I feel it on my face."

All over town, people were wandering outside and squinting in the bright morning light—as if they had spent the entire winter inside. As if they had forgotten the sun.

They met at MacDonnell's.

There were five of them now: Dave, Chan, Billy, Alex, and Dave's little sister, Annie.

Dave was wearing a windbreaker and sneakers. It was the first time he had been outside without boots since November. He felt light and bouncy and full of hope.

"We're going to get him," said Dave.

Billy had a tennis ball.

Billy said, "If we throw the ball at him, maybe he will, you know, get it. And bring it to us. Like fetch."

"He's not going to do that," said Annie, under her breath.

"What?" said Billy. "What did you say?"

"Nothing," said Annie.

Had they been a few years older, had they been teenagers, they would not have been there. Had they been teenagers, they would have been too busy to notice a stray mutt.

Had they been a few years younger, they would have told their parents. Had they been younger, they wouldn't have dreamed this was something they should tackle themselves.

But just like the weather, they were balanced in the precarious no man's land between things. In the fog between fantasy and fact. They had lost the blessings of childhood, but they had not yet received the benedictions of age. They still had this however—they had *the belief of boys*. They assumed the dog needed *them,* and no one else, to come to the rescue. They had come back to do what had to be done.

"I was thinking we should get Ollie," said Chan. Ollie was Chan's dog. "We could tie a rope around Ollie," said Chan, "and send *him* out. To rescue him."

All the boys were nodding. It seemed like a good idea. Until Annie said, "What's he going to do when he gets out there? Untie the rope and hand it to him?"

Everyone stared at her, standing there with her hands in her pockets, the little sister.

"Why is *she* here?" asked Billy.

Dave shot Annie a look. Then he said, "Let's go."

The path to the beach was soft and spongy. They had to jump over the wet spots. So when they got to the shore, they were jumpy and wet.

And when they got there, the dog was gone.

There was nowhere left for him to be. The ice had broken up overnight. There was one small shelf holding the woodshed that still clung to the shore, but all of the broken slabs and chunks that had filled the lake had disappeared. From where they were standing, there was only open water.

Chan said, "We should have told our parents."

They stood there in a gloomy line, staring at the flat surface of the lake.

It was Annie who spotted him.

"There!" she said. "Over there."

Annie was pointing at the far end of the lake.

She was pointing to the bay where the lake empties into the river, and the river passes under the bridge on its way to Little Narrows.

The dog was on a piece of ice no bigger than a fridge. It looked more like a painting of a dog than a dog itself, sitting stiff and upright, and staring straight ahead.

"The falls," said Dave. "We have to get him."

As he said it, the piece of ice the dog was sitting on slipped into the current and began to bob up and down, began to pick up speed.

"Come on," said Dave. He started running. They all peeled off behind him, all five of them, racing for the bridge. Dave in the lead, Annie falling behind.

In summertime, the Little Nation River is a fun place. Kids hike the path that meanders along its west bank and leads down to the falls. In summer, the falls are a place where a kid can play unsupervised. Or could in those days.

The water is always low and lazy in the summer, so you can mess around in the pools, slide down the mossy chute without danger of being washed over. Or little danger.

But in spring, when the river is full and the water is running fast and black, high and cold, kids aren't supposed to go near the falls. Dave knew if they didn't stop that dog before he went into the river, he was going all the way to the falls, and there was no way he, or anyone, was surviving that.

As they ran, it was mud one minute and snow the next, and

every once in a while, a rogue piece of ice, just to remind them they were doing something dangerous.

But no one fell. They got to the bridge, safe and sound and panting. But they got there just as the dog did.

So there was no time to hatch a plan.

They got there just in time to see him bob by—standing on his ice boat, barking and snapping at the white waves jumping around his feet.

They stood on the bridge, leaning on the rail, and watched him pass under, then they ran over to the other side and watched him emerge and bob along, until he disappeared around the corner near the big willow.

"We have to get him," said Dave. "Before the falls. Or he's a goner."

They had a chance.

There was one more bridge, where Macaulay's road crossed the river. If they could get to the Macaulay's bridge before the dog did …

"How we going to do *that?*" said Chan.

"A ride," said Dave. "We need a ride. Come on."

And so they were running again. Back to town, back past Kerrigan's Food, and the hardware, and past MacDonnell's post office and general store, to the Maple Leaf Restaurant, where Dave knew his dad would be having his morning coffee—his truck parked out back.

Annie huffed around the corner as they were climbing into the truck.

"Where's Dad?" asked Annie.

"We're not telling Dad," said Dave. "We can't risk it."

He was right, of course. There are certain things that kids have to look after by themselves. There are certain things that *are* too risky for adults.

If they had got Charlie, Charlie might have driven them to the Macaulay's bridge, though probably not fast enough. But when they got there, he would not have let them get up to what they got up to. He would not have let them execute the plan Dave was starting to formulate.

"Are you out of your mind?" said Annie.

"Probably," said Dave.

"Me too," said Annie and she crawled into the truck.

Even today in Big Narrows, there are people who leave their keys in their cars. These days, they are likely to slip them under the floor mat, but back then, just about everyone left them right in the ignition.

Charlie was no exception.

Dave ruffled Annie's hair and said, "You run the pedals."

And with Annie crouched between Dave's feet, working the gas and the brake, they lurched away.

Billy clutching the emergency brake with all his might. "In case there's an emergency," said Billy.

"More gas," said Dave. "More gas."

They made it, in first gear, the engine screaming the whole way.

They rocked to a stop on the side of the road. Dave opened the door and jumped out.

The first thing he noticed was the roar of the falls in the distance.

The rest of them scrambled out of the car, and they all ran to the bridge and stared up the river.

Dave looked at Annie and said, "We might have missed him. We might be too late, you know."

"We aren't too late," said Annie. "He is coming. What are we going to do?"

There was only one thing to do.

"We have to lower someone over the edge," said Billy.

Everyone stopped what they were doing and stared at Dave.

Dave turned and stared at Annie.

"Give me your belt," said Dave to Chan.

They fashioned a harness out of their belts and grabbed the rope out of the back of the truck.

They fixed the harness around Annie, and then fixed the rope to the harness.

Someone should have said, *Are you sure about this?*

Someone should have said, *This is not a good idea.*

But that's why they didn't bring Charlie.

Anyway, Annie had already climbed over the railing and was standing on the far side of the bridge.

Dave said, "Lean out."

"I'm too scared," said Annie.

Dave said, "Let go of the railing. Shut your eyes and lean."

The dog came floating around the corner.

Dave pointed at it and said, "Annie."

Annie stepped off the edge of the bridge, screaming at the top of her lungs.

There is a time in a person's life when everything changes.

This was Annie's turn.

All her life, she had been Dave's little sister. All her life, she had been the tagalong.

But in that moment, right there, right then, swinging back and forth over the black cold water of the Little Nation River, Annie, not yet ten, came of age.

She let go of the edge of the bridge, and from that moment on, her life was never the same. She was no longer on the sidelines *watching* things happen. Everyone was watching *her*.

But she didn't know any of that yet. All she knew was that she was swaying back and forth over that river like a bucket at the end of a rope, like a YoYo on a string, like a bungee jumper at the end of her jump, swinging and swaying and screaming.

And then the harness shifted and Annie flipped upside down.

She could almost touch the water.

The dog was almost there.

"Now what?" screamed Annie.

Everybody froze. They had forgotten the most important part of the rescue.

The plan.

The dog almost sailed right by her.

But he didn't. As the boys stood there dumbstruck, the dog jumped towards Annie's outstretched arms.

The boys watched it happen in slow motion. The dog hit Annie's chest high. She grabbed on, and so did he.

They didn't *need* a plan. The *dog* had the plan.

Being there, Dave would say years later, is usually the only plan you ever need.

And then he would tell the story of Annie and the bridge and the dog.

But that was years later.

Right now, the only thing on his mind was getting Annie and that mutt onto the bridge.

"Pull," cried Dave.

And they pulled and hauled her up, up and over the railing. When that was done, they stood there on the bridge, looking at each other in shock, and the dog fell to the road. He barked twice, and then walked casually over to the truck and peed on the front tire.

And that was more or less that.

Well, that wasn't completely that. There was still Charlie to deal with.

Charlie was waiting for them in the parking lot of the Maple Leaf Restaurant.

First thing he said to them when they shuddered to a stop in front of him, first thing he said after they got out of the cab and Dave handed him the keys, was, "I was wondering when you'd get back."

They drove down to the dock and parked there and looked over the water. Dave, Annie and Charlie in the front of the cab, the dog sitting next to Annie, licking her hand.

First thing they agreed was that they wouldn't tell their mother.

"It wouldn't be good for her," said Charlie. "She would just worry.

"Now we got to figure out some story about this mutt. And it can't involve ice or bridges. I just don't want to think about that."

"Could we say we got him at the pound?" asked Dave.

"That'd be good," said Charlie. "If we *had* a pound."

So they cooked up a story.

And then Charlie said, "As for you two, you two need to be punished."

Annie said, "But Mom always does that part. You have no experience in that."

"You're right," said Charlie.

"Maybe we could just, you know, pretend," said Charlie.

"I am okay with *that*," said Dave.

"Me too," said Annie.

"Okay," said Charlie. "If it ever gets out, if she ever gets wind of any of this, you *were* punished, right?"

Annie was nodding her head.

"Well," said Charlie, "best we go home then. And introduce this mutt to your mother.

They put a note up at the post office and an announcement in *The Casket*, but they never heard anything, and no one in town could remember ever seeing that dog before.

And so he became theirs.

It was Annie who named him.

"Scout," said Annie. "His name is Scout."

It was a good enough name. It seemed to suit him. And anyway, of all of them, she had earned the right to bestow it. So no one argued.

"Pretty sorry-looking mutt if you ask me," said Charlie.

Supper was over. They were still sitting at the table. Scout was asleep, on the floor, by the stove.

"Doesn't look like he has much life left in him."

Charlie was wrong about that.

Scout lived for ever.

He went on, and on, and on.

As for the woodshed, the woodshed didn't sink that spring. That night, the night they rescued Scout, the piece of ice *it* was on broke away from the shore, and the next morning, the shed floated down the river, or what was left of it floated away. The roof was half–ripped off as it went under the bridge, but Old Man Macaulay saw it go over the falls, and there were other reports of it bobbing along in the flow. A lot of people saw it go through Little Narrows on Monday afternoon.

So there was no winner that year—no one even knows where the last timbers disappeared, or whether they actually even sank.

Annie and Dave had many great springs growing up. But that spring was the best of them. It is the one they talk about when they get together. That day, the one they rescued Scout, especially.

MACAULAY'S MOUNTAIN

It was a mamba. The deadliest snake in the world. It kills one hundred percent of its victims in no time flat. Did it get any venom on you?
—MURPHY

The dirt road that climbs the hill back of Old Man Macaulay's barn, or Macaulay's Mountain as people in the Narrows call it, climbs with a steady and certain resolve. It bisects the mountain like a brown stripe on a green flag.

You wouldn't want to drive it in your *city* car, even though you could make it as far as Macaulay's sugar shack. Above the sugar bush, you wouldn't want to drive *anything* along the road, except maybe a dirt bike or an ATV, although plenty of people go walking up there.

Once you pass the sugar bush, there is grass growing down the middle of the road, and the trees start closing in. It is possible to imagine the day coming when the forest will swallow the road. But it is still a grand place, and you can understand why two boys, walking up there for the first time unsupervised, as Sam and his friend Murphy did this summer, would come away with adventure on their minds.

This is the first summer Sam has been in Big Narrows without Dave and Morley. He is at that awkward age—too young to be left alone, too old to be looked after. And so he went to visit his grandmother, and his best friend, Murphy, went along for the company. The boys stayed with Margaret and her new husband, Smith. They roamed around Big Narrows on two old bikes that Smith found for them—exploring the world in a way they never could have if they had stayed in the city.

Macaulay's Mountain soon became their favourite place. There is so much adventure for boys to find on the mountain— the jumping cliff, the lake, the old ruined cabin—but nothing more exciting than the call to adventure that radiates like waves of heat from the abandoned car that is rusting away, near where the road flattens at the edge of the blueberry field, just before the pond.

Over the years, countless boys have come upon the wreck and have reacted pretty much the same way as Sam and Murphy reacted when *they* came upon it.

Murphy saw it first. He stopped dead in his tracks. His mouth dropped, his heartbeat accelerated.

"What?" asked Sam, looking at his friend. "Ohmigod," said Sam, looking where his friend was pointing.

The car was no more than ten yards away. And both of them were thinking exactly the same thing.

Dead Bodies.

As if one, they took a step backwards.

"It looks like it has been there for years," said Sam.

"Skeletons," said Murphy.

"Zombies," said Sam. "Lost souls."

What more could a boy ask for in the dog days of summer than a half-buried, wrecked car, a whiff of fear, and the possibility of that fear ratcheting into terror.

"A plan," said Murphy. "We need a plan."

And so they worked out a plan, driven more by curiosity than bravery. One of them would approach the car. The other would hang back, so if anything bad happened, *he* could go for help.

"Who?" said Sam.

"Me," said Murphy. "I run faster. If something happens, I can run for help."

"You can't run faster," said Sam. "I can beat you anytime."

They flipped a coin.

And so it was Sam who carried the stick they dug out of the forest, swinging it by his thigh like a club as he walked, ever so carefully, towards the car. The blueberry field suddenly still. His feet crunching the gravel on the road. His heart pounding. His body half turned in case he had to bolt.

"Careful," said Murphy, ready to bolt himself.

It was like something from a movie. The moment when the hero confronts the great fearful thing, the beast, the mountain, the werewolf. Or in this case, what was left of a 1948 Studebaker Land Cruiser.

The car once belonged to Peter Macaulay, the *older* of the two Macaulay brothers. Peter put the car in the ditch on an October night in the 1960s. He had planned to pull it out, but it snowed that night. The snow didn't melt, and that meant the car had to stay on the mountain until spring. And that was the spring Peter Macaulay was killed. No one could believe it at the time. Peter, so full of life. So full of adventure. Peter, who everyone knew would one day take over the Macaulay farm— until he died on it. Peter, dead and gone.

No one had the heart to move the car that summer, or the next one, and then Peter's father, the original Old Man

Macaulay, passed on himself. And so the car stayed put, a rusting memorial to Peter and his lost youth.

The present owner of the Macaulay farm, the latest Old Man Macaulay, is actually Peter's younger brother, Garth. Garth was in the car the night Peter put it in the ditch. And he was driving the tractor the afternoon the combine killed him.

The car was all Garth had left of his brother. He liked that it was up there by the field. He never made any effort to move it.

Any useful bits from the engine had been long scavenged, and the windows shot out by hunters. But the steering wheel was still there, and remarkably, the car still had tires.

Sam peered in the passenger-side window.

"It's empty," he said.

"Back seat?" said Murphy.

"Empty," said Sam.

"What about *under* the seats?" asked Murphy.

"I can't *see* under the seats," said Sam.

"Look under the seats," said Murphy.

"I'd have to open the door," said Sam. And he walked back and handed Murphy the stick and said, "*You* look under the seats."

Murphy rolled his eyes and said, "Do I have to do everything?"

There was nothing under the seats. And soon enough, they were sitting in the car. Murphy was in the driver's seat, Sam beside him, in the same seat where Garth Macaulay was sitting that October night so long ago. Murphy had his hands on the steering wheel.

"If we could get it out of the ditch," said Murphy, "we could drive it down the mountain."

He was trying to jerk the wheel to the left and right, leaning forward and peering out over the hood, turning around, checking his blind spot.

Then he let the wheel go, reached out and opened the glove compartment. There was a snake sleeping in there. It fell into Sam's lap.

The boys are both still young. Over the years, their legs will grow, and their muscles will lengthen and strengthen. They will become more coordinated and graceful. But they will never move faster, ever, in their lives, than they did at that moment, that afternoon on Macaulay's Mountain, when the glove compartment opened and the snake fell out. Never in their lives.

"It was in my lap," said Sam when they stopped running about two hundred yards down the road. "It was a rattler and it was in my lap."

"It wasn't a rattler," said Murphy. "It was a mamba. The deadliest snake in the world. It kills one hundred percent of its victims in no time flat. Did it get any venom on you?"

It was half an hour before they were able to summon the resolve to return. They didn't *want* to. They *had* to. The idea of being behind the wheel of that car with the wind in their hair was too good.

"Wouldn't we need to have our licenses?" asked Sam.

They were back in the front seat. Murphy shook his head. He pointed out the window.

Murphy said, "That isn't technically a road. *This* isn't a car—technically. There's no engine. It is a wreck. You don't need a license to drive a wreck."

"My father has a license," said Sam. "He drives a wreck."

"The trick," said Murphy, "is going to be getting it out of the ditch."

"How fast do you think it will go?" asked Sam.

They were circling the car. Murphy was squatting down on his haunches, peering at the back wheels.

Murphy said, "We're going to need a jack, and a pulley, and some boards. We can jack it up, put the boards under the wheels, and pull it out."

It was Sam who found the crowbar. Lying on the front bumper. It was Murphy who said they should pry open the trunk.

"There could be a jack in there," said Murphy.

He never imagined there would be a pulley too.

They found a pile of boards near the old cabin by the lake. By the time they gathered everything up, it was time for supper.

"We have to go," said Sam.

They went back the next morning. Standing up on their bikes, pumping, leaning left and then right, one side to the other. Through town, over the old bridge and past all the little farms, all the clothes on all the clotheslines, all the wood stacked by all the sheds.

They worked at it all morning. At noon they sat on the roof of the car and ate their lunch. Their shirts were off, their faces stained with mud and sweat.

"Soon," said Murphy.

"If we get it all the way down," said Sam, "we could fix it up, and when we get our licenses, we would have our own car."

They had never worked with such concentration and determination in their young lives. If they worked half that hard, a quarter that hard, at school, they would skip grades. They would win scholarships and medals. They would go to Harvard or Oxford or God knows where.

But schoolwork doesn't involve sleeping snakes, or old cars, or the promise of great adventure. They ate their lunch, and they slid off the roof, the smell of the sun on their skinny arms, and they got back at it. Jacking the wheels one by one and shoring them up with the wood they had found by the cabin.

And slowly, incredibly, unbelievably, they got it done.

All four wheels, up and clear.

"Okay," said Murphy.

"Okay," said Sam.

They had the pulley wrapped around a tree on the far side of the road.

"Slowly," said Murphy. "Slowly."

And slowly the car came. With slow and certain determination it came out of the ditch until, before they knew it, they had it on the road, lined up and pointing down the slope, with a log across the front wheels to stop it from rolling away on them.

"Are you ready?" said Murphy.

Murphy was standing on the road by the passenger-side bumper.

"Ready," said Sam.

There were no seat belts. Sam was lashed into the driver's seat with the rope they had brought. He was wearing ski goggles.

"Three," said Murphy.

"Are you sure you can do this?" said Sam.

"Two," said Murphy.

"Just get out of the way," said Sam.

"One," said Murphy.

And he yanked the log from in front of the wheels.

Nothing happened.

Sam said, "Nothing is happening."

Murphy ran to the back of the car to give it a push. But before he was halfway there, the car was moving by itself, rolling down the road. Slowly.

It was slow enough that Murphy was able to easily swing himself into the passenger seat, tie himself in place, and put on *his* goggles.

They were going faster now. How fast? Depends who you ask.

Let's just say, a lot faster than you would want your begoggled son or daughter going down the side of a mountain lashed into a 1948 Studebaker Land Cruiser.

Sam shouted, "Which one is the brake pedal?"

Murphy said, "There are no brakes."

Sam said, "How are we going to stop it then?"

Murphy said, "I'm working on that. Just get us around this corner."

They made it around the corner. And the next one.

But not the third. That was surprising because they were actually slowing down. Coming onto a long flat stretch, the front wheel caught the ditch, and Sam lost control, and then, well … If you could get *them* to tell you about it, they would both swear they were airborne, that they left the road, hit the ground with a mighty *thwack* and shuddered to a stop.

"Yowzas!" said Sam. "How fast were we going?"

"A hundred," said Murphy. "Maybe two."

They untied themselves, and they got out. They stood on the side of the road.

Sam said, "This is the best day of my entire life."

It was only when they got back to their bikes that it occurred to them that they might have done something wrong.

"Joyriding," said Sam.

"Grand theft auto," said Murphy.

"If they catch us, they'll send us to *juvie*."

They went back up the mountain, took off their shirts and wiped the car from top to bottom.

"Everywhere we touched it," said Murphy.

And then they went back down, got their bikes and pedalled home.

They talked it over, backwards and forwards, inside and out. They lasted a day and a half before they told anyone.

Two days after their ride on the mountain, they went to the police station. They stood by the door, uncertainly.

Police chief and sole member of the Big Narrows Police Force Revlyn Kavanagh was sitting at his desk, preoccupied with a bowl of his wife's homemade corn chowder.

"Come on in, boys," he said, when he spotted them. "What can I do for you?"

"We are here to report a crime," said Sam.

"Theft under," said Murphy. "Joyriding, and driving a vehicle with an obliterated ID."

"I beg your pardon?" said Revlyn, reaching for his statute book. He looked confused.

"Section 354.2," said Murphy.

Revlyn glanced at his half-finished soup mournfully and said, "We better go check this out, boys."

When they got outside, he said, "You leave your bikes here. We'll go in the squad car.

"I am afraid you boys are going to have to ride in back. Procedure."

Once they were out of town, he put on the siren and the flashing red light. Sam and Murphy, sitting in the back seat, as white as ghosts.

No one said much as they walked up the mountain, past the sugar shack and the trail to the jumping cliff, around the corner to the big rock and up the little rise. Sam and Murphy's little hearts were pounding. And then around the next corner to the ditch.

The car was gone.

"It was right here," said Murphy.

"There," said Sam, pointing.

But it wasn't.

It wasn't there at all.

They kept climbing. Around the three corners, up the long slow hill, Revlyn taking off his hat and wiping the sweat from his brow.

And there it was. Where it had always been. Where they had found it that first afternoon. Where it had been for all those years since that night in October when Peter Macaulay drove it off the road with his brother Garth sitting at his side.

"Boys," said Chief Kavanagh, shaking his head, and pointing at the car, "it doesn't look like we have a crime here."

"But you can see the dirt," said Sam, "by the wheels, where we dug it up."

"You can see where we dug it up," said Murphy.

"Boys," said Chief Kavanagh. "What I see is a 1948 Studebaker Land Cruiser sitting in the same place where it has sat for some fifty years. I think you boys are in the clear."

He drove them back to town. They got on their bikes and rode out of town slowly. They stopped on the Thamesville Bridge, took the path down, and sat on the riverbank, throwing sticks in the water while they tried to figure it out.

"It happened," said Sam. "We did it."

"I don't know," said Murphy. "There are many cases of socio-psychological phenomena mentioned in the literature where people are convinced of things that have never happened. Vampires and satanic possession to name two. It's just mass hysteria."

"We aren't hysterical," said Sam. "We did it. Someone took it back."

They will never know the truth of it.

Murphy will never go back to the mountain. But Sam will, and every time he goes up there, he will tell the person, or the people, he is with about those three days that summer.

And they will make their own guesses as to what happened. But no one will get it right.

Peter's brother Garth, Old Man Macaulay, knows a whole lot more than anyone else about that car slowly rusting away on the side of the road, slowly disappearing itself. But even he doesn't know all of it.

He knows that Sam and Murphy found the ropes and the pulley that he left in the trunk, especially for boys like them. And he knows that over the decades, five other pairs of boys have done the same thing—found the things he left and figured out how to use them to get his brother's car out of the ditch and ride it down the mountain one more time.

He always knows when they are at it, and he is always there with his tractor to pull the car back up the hill and set it back where it belongs. And when he has done that, he inflates the tires, and puts the rubber snake back in the glove compartment, reassured in some strange way that his brother left something behind that still gives people joy.

He knows that part, but even he doesn't know it all. He doesn't know, for instance, that Stephen Kerrigan and Megan Lorius were sitting in the back seat of his brother's old car on the summer evening that Stephen proposed to Megan; or that Bernadette Armstrong spent a night in it some forty years ago, when she was a young mother in her early thirties, thinking about leaving Alfred. She had decided the next morning, as the sun rose over the mountain, that she loved him too much to do that. She deserved better. But she resolved to *do* better instead. And she had a good cry and walked down the mountain, feeling the better for it.

These things *he* doesn't know, these moments, fading like old photographs, like the memory of his brother, Peter, who left the car at the edge of the blueberry fields near the top of the mountain and vanished himself before he could get it back. All these things hover in the air up there, while the forest closes in, and the car sits in the filtered sun, rusting away.

TOUR DE DAVE

You can't be serious. A twelve-thousand-dollar bike?
—BERNIE

Most people, if they decide to take up a hobby, slip into it gradually. Often it takes decades. You do something as a child—someone gives you a model plane for Christmas or teaches you how to knit—and something happens. A synapse fires, a switch is flipped, a path is laid down. There is something about the setting of the glue or the clicking of the needles that pleases you, something that fills some big, deep void. Something that you might have difficulty putting into words—but you know.

When things like that happen, they don't go away. They might be forgotten, they might become buried by life's hurly-burly, but things that are buried have a habit of rising to the surface.

Everything surfaces eventually.

And so the boy, toy hammer in hand, who stands beside his father and watches him at work, grows up and builds a small deck, or fixes some drywall, and before you know it, he is renovating houses. The girl, who helps her mother with the weekend weeding, becomes the woman who pores over seed catalogues on dark winter evenings, counting the days until the sun warms the dark earth.

Mostly it is obvious where the echoes come from, but for

some of us, they appear out of nowhere. Some of us answer more mysterious calls. We are summoned to action the way the lesser species are summoned to migrate. But if the path is less clear, the commitment to action is no less enthusiastic. We may have no understanding of the wherefore or the why, but when the call comes, we follow.

Dave's enthusiasms have most often been of the latter type. They seem to erupt out of nowhere. His neighbour, Ted Anderson, falls into the first camp. Ted, who is both slow and methodical, is a man who understands the joy of delayed pleasure and the important rhythms of baby steps.

It might not come as a surprise then, that when Dave's interests intersected with Ted's, the results were not satisfying for either of them.

Because things began with Ted, they began slowly. They began with a birthday present from his wife, Polly. It was his fortieth birthday, so Polly thought long and hard about what she should give him.

Of course, when you think long and hard about a gift for someone you love, and after deep thought, give them something you think might please them, you always run the risk of giving them something that could please them way too much.

That's the danger with the perfect presents, sometimes they can become ... perfectly horrible.

So it was, the year Ted turned forty, that Polly snuck out to the garage in the dark of the night, tied a red bow to the handlebars of the bike she had hidden out there, pushed it awkwardly through the dark kitchen and into the living room, and leaned it against the couch for Ted to find the next morning.

It was a modest bike. Three speeds and a canvas saddlebag. Ted often talked about his first two-wheeler—the bike he got the year he turned four. Polly was thinking Ted might enjoy riding again—maybe even to the market on Saturday mornings.

Because Ted didn't know any better, the bike made him modestly happy. And in the spring, to show his appreciation, he began riding to work the odd few mornings—when the weather was warm and the roads were dry. And that was more or less that.

For more or less a year.

Until something happened, and Polly realized her understanding of her husband's desires was more sophisticated than she had imagined.

Today, some ten years later, Ted owns seven bikes.

They hang from hooks in a sparkling row in his basement, as if he were running a bike store down there.

Closest to the door, there is his go-to machine: a classic Italian road bike, a Pinarello, with a leather saddle, drop handlebars and Campy components. It is the bike Ted uses to get around.

Beside the Pinarello? Its polar opposite: a three-speed Dutch bike Ted uses when it is snowing.

Next, is the off-road Trek. It's Ted's only American bike—his homage to Lance Armstrong.

And beside that, in the place of honour, is his pride and joy, his *racing* bike—a baby blue, artisan-built, carbon-fibre Torelli. It cost him $12,000. Everything on the Torelli is handmade, right down to the $200 ultralight carbon-fibre water bottle.

It's all about saving weight, shaving grams. It's what you do if you are a serious cyclist. And Ted is serious.

Ted made the leap from riding to racing over three or four years. Today it is nothing for Ted to come home on a weeknight, jump on his bike and go for a fifty-kilometre ride. Every Sunday he hauls the bike out to the country and hammers out a century—which is what Ted calls going one hundred *miles*.

He always starts and finishes with an espresso at Kenny Wong's café, Wong's Scottish Meat Pies.

He doesn't *have* to go to Kenny's. He has his own espresso machine at home. But since Kenny got *his* machine, dropping in has become Ted's ritual.

He likes it there, likes to tell Kenny the latest about his bike. Or if Kenny is busy, anyone else who makes the mistake of looking remotely interested. He says being on the Torelli is more like dancing than riding. He says he and his bike know each other so well they react to each other's moods.

"It is like it has a personality," he was saying to a man who sat down beside him the other day. "There are times when the bike is in control of me. When I'm not even steering. Like I'm just along for the ride."

When it comes to biking, Ted has the enthusiasm of a convert. He is not a proponent of cycling. He is a proselytizer. He is not an enthusiast. He is an evangelist.

"Think of it as an investment," he preached to Bernie Schellenberger one afternoon, his empty espresso cup in front of him.

"You can't be serious," said Bernie. "A twelve-thousand-dollar bike?"

"An investment in your health," said Ted.

Bernie rolled his eyes.

And then Ted pounced.

"Bikes don't depreciate the way cars do," said Ted.

Bernie had just bought a new car.

Ted has a preacher's knack for zeroing in on people's weak spots.

"A bike is the very best way to unwind," he once told Mary Turlington. "I always insist Polly go for a ride when she gets as grumpy as you get. It always calms her down."

He believes he is doing them a favour.

But when Ted talks about his bike, he manages to make just about everyone in the neighbourhood feel bad about themselves.

Everyone, strangely, except for Dave.

"Have you ever *felt* his bike?" Dave asked Kenny one day. "You can lift it off the ground with one finger. It's as light as a piece of paper. I can't imagine what it would be like to ride it."

Which was a lie. Dave had spent altogether too much time imagining what it might be like to ride Ted's bike. He had imagined leaning into a corner. Riding the wind. Standing up. Swaying side to side. He had imagined *feeling* the road beneath him.

So one Saturday afternoon, when Dave came upon a yard sale and spotted a set of racing gear for sale—the spandex shorts, the colourful jersey, the helmet and gloves—he bought the lot of it.

He even bought himself a pair of cycling shoes.

The guy selling the stuff couldn't have been nicer.

"You have to watch these," he said, flipping over one of the black leather shoes. He showed Dave the silver cleat on the sole and explained how it locked onto the pedal.

"Like a ski boot locks onto a ski," he said.

Then he said, "Be careful walking around. They can be slippery on hard surfaces."

When Dave left, he owned everything a cyclist would need. Except, of course, the bike.

But before an expenditure of that magnitude, it's good to do a little research, to get a *feel* for the thing, to push your dreams against the wheel of reality.

Dave tried to bring the idea up with Ted. Not directly. He hinted about it. Would Ted loan his bike to someone, say for a weekend, or something? Ted looked so horrified Dave dropped the topic right away.

But he kept thinking if he could get even fifteen minutes on the bike, he'd be able to tell if he would like it.

And then one morning he spotted Ted's car parked in the lane behind his store. He knew it was Ted's car because Ted's bike was on the roof rack.

Dave ran upstairs and changed into his bike clothes. The whole kit. And he tiptoed carefully out to the alley in his cycling shoes, just the way the guy had showed him.

He knew he had time for this. Ted was at Kenny's, having his coffee.

Dave wasn't going to take the bike *off* the car and go for a *ride*. He just wanted to sit on it.

So he tiptoed into the alley and he climbed up onto the roof of Ted's car. He swung himself onto the saddle of Ted's pride and joy, and he leaned over the handlebars, feeling amazingly good. This *was* something he could do. He could *totally* do this.

Dave waved his hands over his head—just like the guys in the Tour de France.

And *that* was when Ted walked out the back door of the restaurant. Dave had his hands over his head. Ted had his head down, staring at a map. And Dave thought, *okay, okay*. He could get off the bike and slip down the other side of the car before Ted saw him. He shifted all his weight onto his right foot so he could step off the bike.

There was an ominous *click*.

The pedal grabbed the cleat on his shoe, just like the man told him it would. Like a ski grabbing a ski boot. And it wouldn't let go.

Dave pushed with the other foot.

There was a second *click*. Then Dave heard the car door slam. And the engine start.

The car began rolling down the alley.

This was a Sunday morning. Ted was heading to the country.

Dave was perched on his roof. He looked like the space shuttle bolted on top of a 747.

Ted pulled out of the alley and onto the street right in front of a taxi. The taxi driver pointed at Ted's roof and shouted.

This was not unusual.

This happens to Ted frequently. People who know bikes often point at his roof. Ted smiled at the cabbie and waved back. Then he stepped on the gas and pulled away.

More than the usual number of people honked their horns that morning. Each time they did, Ted smiled proudly and honked back, while Dave clung on for dear life.

Dave couldn't believe what was happening. He couldn't believe that Ted was ignoring all of the pointing and waving drivers who were clearly trying to save Dave's life. He should have screamed for help when the car was taking off and Ted might have heard him. Now he had to use every ounce of his energy to hang on—to stay alert. He was terrified. What would happen if he fainted?

As they continued to pick up speed, Dave's hair was pushed back by the wind. His mouth froze open. He looked like a kid on a roller coaster. But not one of the happy ones.

When Ted hit the highway, the bike's wheels began to turn in the wind. Dave had to pedal to keep up. Pretty soon Dave was pedalling his heart out. He actually looked like one of the guys in the Tour de France. But not one of the happy ones.

Unfortunately Ted's bike rack hadn't been designed for Dave's added weight. It began to work loose.

As they flew along, Dave started to sway from side to side on the roof.

Panic can be a wonderful thing. It can help you get a lot done in a short period of time. Often, without a lot of thought.

Dave, who had been twisting his feet this way and that, was finally seized completely by panic and twisted one of his feet the correct way.

His right foot flew free. It was caught by the wind and began flapping behind him like a sock on a clothesline.

The other foot popped out almost immediately. It flapped around too.

For a moment, Dave lost track of the gravity of his situation. He turned and stared in amazement at his legs flapping behind him.

He had no idea he was that flexible.

And then he did the only thing he could think of doing. With an enormous effort, he managed to hoist his left leg over the frame and rest it on the roof of the car. Clinging onto the bike like a wing-walker from the days of the barnstorming biplanes, he moved his right foot down too.

His colourful jersey flapped in the wind as he dropped down to his knees and grabbed the straps that held the bike rack to the roof.

He began to inch his way towards the front windshield.

This wasn't the first time Dave's enthusiasms had stranded him on a roof. As a young parent, he had climbed onto the roof of his own home to put up the Christmas lights, working alone in a misguided attempt to be first in the neighbourhood. He had ended up with his tongue frozen to the TV antenna.

Other infatuations, or manias as Morley liked to call them, had led him down equally bumpy, if not as perilous, paths.

Like the Christmas when, trying to turn his yard white, he had iced his neighbours into their home with the artificial snow-making machine; or the autumn he tried to raise his own turkey; or the toilet-trained cat that wouldn't stop flushing the toilet. The list went on and on.

But none of his enthusiasms had ever courted death this way. Dear God. Ted was speeding up. *This* was how he was going to die.

He reached out and grabbed the frame of the front windshield and pulled himself forward another inch.

Below him, and oblivious to the drama on his roof, Ted was having the time of his life. Ted was driving down the road without a care in the world. He was listening to his all-time favourite album: *The Best of John Denver*. Tapping the steering wheel and singing along with the music: "Take Me Home, Country Roads."

He was just coming to the chorus, when out of nowhere, there was a face staring at him through his windshield.

An upside-down face obscuring his vision.

Take me home, insisted John Denver.

"No!" screamed Ted.

Ted slammed on the brakes.

A number of things happened at once.

The paper-light, baby blue Torelli lifted off the roof and floated up in the air like a feather. It seemed to hover there for a moment. Then it hit the pavement just in front of Ted's front wheels.

He barely felt it as he rolled over it.

At that exact instant, Dave, who had a death grip on the rack's straps, flipped over the windshield and landed on the hood.

And the car screeched to a stop.

Ted immediately understood what had happened. It was his worst nightmare. He had hit a cyclist. The cyclist looked strangely familiar.

Time heals many wounds. Dave quietly dropped his cycling clothes in a Goodwill box the next week.

Ted got himself a new bike with the insurance money. He doesn't talk about the new bike nearly as much as he talked about the old one. If you press him, he will tell you that he still feels a good bike can be a man's salvation. But that really depends on whom Ted is talking to. Ted has discovered the problem with proselytizing: when you preach, you never know who your converts will be.

THE HOUSE NEXT DOOR

*It's not exactly a fish. Well, it is a fish. But it is also an art piece.
Anyway. Fish or art, who knows, it needs to be fed.*
—JO

They moved into the neighbourhood two years ago. In the autumn. Into the Tomlinson place. No one knew anything about them before they arrived, not even the Tomlinsons. All Joe could say was they seemed nice enough—a young couple, no kids, but probably they *would* have kids. Time for some young blood on the street. A renewal.

Joe and Millie had renewed *themselves* into one of those condos by the water, thirty-seventh floor.

"Our kids are gone," said Millie.

"Wait until you see it," said Joe.

"You can see forever," said Millie.

The new people had a dog. The first evidence Dave saw of them *was* the dog. Then the wife jogging along behind it. She was wearing a stretchy running outfit—grey with yellow piping.

It was the day after they moved in. Dave reported the sighting as soon as Morley got home.

"A black dog," he said. "About the size of Arthur. She looked ..." He was talking about the wife now, not the dog, and he almost said *pretty*. She looked pretty. At the last moment he thought better of that.

Instead of *pretty,* he decided to say *nice.* She looked *nice.* But pretty was already halfway out his mouth. It came out *price.*

"She looked price?" said Morley.

"Uh. *Price-y,*" said Dave. Not missing a beat. "She was wearing one of those stretchy jogging outfits."

Now *that* was a professional move, thought Dave. That was *smooth.*

Except Morley was shaking her head.

"Amateur move," said Morley.

Luckily for Dave, the phone rang.

"I'll get it," said Dave, jumping up from the table.

The Turlingtons had everyone over for a barbecue to welcome the new couple. They seemed charming. Maybe she was a bit ... enthusiastic. A little ... smiley. But not unpleasant. Her name was Joanne.

"Jo," she said, hand extended. She was in publishing. Publicity. She told stories about authors they had read: Malcolm Gladwell, Tom Clancy and the British guy, the spy guy.

"John le Carré," said Jo.

She had toured with him. Twice. She called him David.

"Le Carré's a pen name," she said. "His real name is David Cornwell. He likes Indian food. Curries."

"I like her," said Dave, when they got home.

Morley was less effusive.

"Name-dropper," said Morley. "You don't go on and on about all the people *you've* worked with. And you've worked with just as many interesting people as she has." Then she said, "And he seems a little … precious, don't you think?"

He was a corporate lawyer. Real estate stuff. Jordon. Jordon and Jo. J and J.

The dog was Millie.

"Now that is just *weird*," said Morley when Joanne had told her the dog's name.

"The people you bought from," said Morley, "The Tomlinsons. They were *Joe* and …"

"I know," said Jo. "What are the chances of that?"

When she wasn't telling stories about her famous authors, Jo told stories about her dog. Mostly about how dumb she was.

Or that's how the stories started. In the end they were usually about Jordon, her husband, and how dumb *he* was. By the time she got to the end of her story, Millie, the dog, usually looked smart.

"Did you notice," said Morley, "that the husband was the butt of every story?"

"I thought she was charming," said Dave. "It didn't strike me that she really thought he was dumb."

Anyway, they met them at the Turlingtons' barbecue and saw them at a few other neighbourhood events, but barely. As far as Dave and Morley could figure, they were away a lot. Her more than him. Millie, the dog, was picked up each morning by a guy in white overalls. He drove a van. *Casa de Canine. Number one in the city—organic meals, Pilates.*

"*Dinks*," said Morley one night, "They're *dinks*. Double income, no kids."

"They love that dog," said Dave.

"You watch," said Morley. "They are going to start renovating, any day."

They started in the spring.

"Wo-hoo," said Morley .

"You called that," said Dave.

It wasn't one of those upgrade-the-kitchen-cabinets-and-do-the-windows renovations.

By the second summer, the Tomlinson place looked completely different. Nobody had been inside, but from the outside, it looked as if the Tomlinsons had taken their house with them when they left, and Jordon and Jo had built a different one in its place. A modern one.

"You know what this must be costing?" said Morley.

She was standing on the sidewalk with Mary Turlington. They were watching two guys in canvas jackets drop some sort of dwarf tree in the centre of the newly gravelled-over yard.

She didn't say it bitterly. Her feelings were more complicated than that. Part of it was she was put off. Something about these people irked her. Part of it was the extent of the reno—as if the neighbourhood wasn't good enough the way it was.

Mary Turlington, on the other hand, was straightforward envious.

"I know," said Mary, wistfully. "They must have spent a fortune."

"Dave called it the first night," said Morley. "*Pri-ceee.*"

Then one afternoon, around five, the doorbell rang. Morley was home alone, fixing supper. And there was Joanne, standing on the stoop.

"Hello," said Morley, "come in. Come in."

She immediately regretted saying that, thinking to herself, *why did I say that?*

She was embarrassed because coming into Dave and Morley's house is, quite frankly, a bit of a challenge.

You have to really *want* to get in—through the front door anyway. There are shoes everywhere. And shopping bags and backpacks and junk mail. And while you are stepping over and around the shoes and backpacks, you have to avoid the coats protruding from the wall hooks, hanging from the banister and draped over the hall table. To get from the front door to the relative safety of the living room, you have to slither down the hall like a surgical scope.

Morley didn't actually mean for Joanne to come all the way in—certainly not all the way to the living room. That part happened inadvertently. They couldn't stand comfortably in the front hall, so once she was through the door, they shuffled along the hall, where things got worse and worse until, before Morley knew what was happening, they had passed the living room and were in the kitchen staring at the cat, who was standing on the counter, drinking out of the sink.

"I wasn't intending on actually coming in," said Joanne.

I wasn't intending on it either, thought Morley.

But there they were.

And Joanne was telling her how she and Jordon were going away for three weeks—to Italy. Tuscany, Cinque Terre, Rome. The dog was going to the Casa de Canine.

But there was a fish.

"It's Jordon's fish" said Jo. "A gift from a client. It's not *exactly* a fish. Well, it *is* a fish. But it is also an art piece.

Anyway. Fish or art, who knows, it needs to be fed. And I was wondering ..."

She was going to say she was wondering if she could hire their boy to look after it. But before she said anything more, Morley, anxious to get to the point, jumped in.

"I would be delighted," said Morley.

And that is how Morley came to be the first one in the neighbourhood to go inside Joanne and Jordon's house.

It was, simply put, out of this world, unlike any house Morley had ever been in. She had seen pictures in magazines, but nothing like this.

Nothing like this because, well, first off, it was, effectively—empty.

Not *literally* empty. There *was* stuff there. But "empty" is the sense it gave you.

It was, face to face, nose to nose, eyeball to eyeball, the calm to Morley's storm, the up to her down, the ying to her yang ... It was the counter-, the contra-, the—*oh my God, look at that!* There was a big empty table in the foyer, with one, solitary, exquisite flower placed artfully in the middle.

"Don't worry about the orchid," said Jo. "It is going to the conservatory."

"It's ... stunning," said Morley.

The orchid was white.

The floors were grey—polished concrete. *Heated* polished concrete. There was one couch in the living room. One. A linen sectional—ivory.

The ceilings were high, the walls empty—except the wall beside the gas fireplace. On that wall, there was a huge, larger-than-life photograph, a head-and-shoulders, formal portrait of their dog. She was wearing a scarf and a top hat.

The fish was in the den.

The fish was gold.

A *gold* fish in a see-through wall safe.

"It is supposed to be funny," said Jo.

There was a package of frozen bloodworms in the stainless steel, stand-up freezer. Imported from Iceland. The worms, that is. The freezer came from Denmark.

As she walked home, Morley was imagining how she was going to describe the place to Dave. Chewing over words she might use: *Modern. Contemporary. Minimalist.*

It was certainly that.

She said it out loud as she walked onto her porch. "*Minimalist.*" It implied just the right degree of sophistication.

"Minimalist," she said again, feeling pretty sophisticated herself, just for having been there.

Then she reached out to let herself in and the front doorknob came off in her hand.

A few days later, at work, Morley was trying to describe the house. It was lunchtime. There were three of them sitting in her office, eating. Morley was sitting on her desk.

"The bathroom," said Morley, "I am not sure I can *do* the bathroom."

"Take your time," said Darren.

Three nights she had been going there, and she had only just found the bathroom.

"It's not like I'm snooping," she said.

"Why not?" said Darren. "For God's sake, *snoop.*"

So she told them about the bathroom.

"Well. It's big," she said. "Imagine a bedroom. A good-sized bedroom. Now empty it out. And dim the lights."

She was clearly into the bathroom.

"I am not sure," she said, "that there were flowers. But imagine … flowers. Modern. *Minimalist*. The walls are grey. And there are seven shower heads, one on top and then two rows—aimed at your body. And it is in the corner, no stall. It's a *wet* room. And in the middle …"

She had put her sandwich down and had her eyes closed. She could see it perfectly. The tub. In the middle of the room. Not tucked apologetically into the corner. Maybe the most beautiful thing she had ever seen.

"An *infinity* tub. Big enough for two. A perfect rectangle. With a rim around the edge so you can fill it completely to the top and the water pours over the rim and into a gutter."

Morley went over every night after supper. The first few nights, she fed the fish, then left. In and out. The third night, the night she saw the bathroom, was also the night that she sat on the sectional. Just for a moment. Just to see what it felt like. There was a design magazine on the glass coffee table. She sat down. She picked up the magazine and leafed through it. But not for long.

The next night, she brought a book.

"Just one chapter," she said.

Sitting on the sofa reading wasn't snooping, after all.

By the end of the week, she had decided she could spend an hour, but no more. It wasn't snooping. It was house-sitting.

Anyway, whatever it was, it was probably a good idea if it looked as if people were living in the house.

She sat on the couch under a cashmere throw she found in the den.

The thing was, without the clutter of her things around her, Morley felt completely relaxed.

It was so tranquil.

She glanced at *their* couch when she got home. There was a week's worth of newspapers piled at one end. No wonder she felt the weight of the world settling on her.

The next Monday, as she was heading out the door, a smile on her face, and a skip in her step, there was Dave.

"What are you doing over there?" he asked. "Seems to be taking you longer every night. Exactly how many fish are there?"

"I have been taking my book," said Morley.

She stared at him across the kitchen. He was standing between a basket of dirty laundry and a half-unloaded dishwasher.

"Okay," she said, "you can come. But we're not snooping, and we're not staying."

"I have been sitting here," said Morley, pointing at the couch.

Dave picked up a remote control and pointed it at the fireplace. It flared on.

"Dave," said Morley.

He grinned and shrugged his shoulders. *Come on.*

"Well," said Morley. "Okay. But just for five minutes."

And so Dave began going over with her. After supper they would do the dishes, and then head over. Without talking about it, they were establishing a routine.

On Saturday Dave flipped on the fireplace and produced a bottle of wine from his coat. Morley was already curled up on the sectional.

"Just one glass," said Morley.

On Sunday Dave produced cheese and a baguette. As he flipped on the fireplace, Morley said, "Last time."

"Really," she said, half an hour later. "Last time."

It was past eleven when she said, "We should go." She didn't sound convinced.

On Monday Sam said, "What are you guys doing over there anyway?"

Morley said, "Just checking on the fish."

Sam said, "It takes *two of you* to look after a fish?"

Morley said, "Okay. You can come. But no snooping. And just ten minutes. We're not staying."

While she fed the fish, Sam explored the basement.

When he came upstairs, he said, "There's a sauna. Can we use the sauna?"

"No," said Morley. "No, no. We're not using anything here. We're just taking care of the fish."

It's not that the idea hadn't crossed *her* mind. Not to use the sauna, mind you. Morley had been thinking about the infinity tub.

She had stood by the door of the upstairs bathroom and imagined herself fully immersed, surrounded by candles, water trickling over the sides.

"We can't just move in here," she said. As she said it, she sat down on the sofa and picked up a piece of the pâté Dave had brought.

"We are just looking after the fish," she said. "We can't treat this place like our own."

She had considered how nice it would be if they *could* move in. So that every time she flushed a toilet, she wouldn't have to jiggle the toilet handle until she heard something in the tank go clunk. So she would have a stove where all the burners worked on all the settings, not just the back left one. So she could move through a house where every door frame, every wall, every floor wasn't nicked, cut, scratched and scuffed.

Truthfully, in her heart of hearts, she wanted her house to look like a house that her family didn't live in.

All good things must come to an end.

Jordon and Jo were due back on Saturday evening.

On Friday after dinner, Morley said she was going to go over by herself.

"Party's over," she said.

Dave said, "What's in the backpack?"

Morley said, "Cleaning stuff."

She unpacked as soon as she got there. A dozen candles, a hair dryer, a terrycloth robe, two towels and a bottle of bright bath salts.

She hadn't said *what* was going to get cleaned.

She fed the fish. Then she carried the stuff upstairs and stared at the tub.

It was a foolish idea. She knew better. She wasn't actually going to do it. She said that out loud.

"I'm not going to do it," she said.

As she said it, she was arranging the candles at the foot of the tub.

It is hard to describe a moment of complete perfection. But that night, lying in the steaming tub, surrounded by the flickering light of her candles, might be as close as Morley has ever come. She sank into the benevolence of the water and felt herself floating away in a world of warm oils, mysterious fragrances and silk curtains billowing in the wind.

She thought it would be good. But it was better than anything she had ever imagined.

A blissful hour later, she was wrapped in her white robe, blow-drying her hair, lost in the wonder of it all, when Joanne and Jordon came home.

The hair dryer was so loud that Morley didn't hear the door open.

Joanne came in first. Jordon was still outside, paying the taxi, getting the bags. So it was Jo who came in, heard a noise that sounded familiar but strange at the same time, and came upstairs. Joanne walked into the bedroom, and stood by the bed, staring at the sight of Morley, her back to the door, wrapped in her white robe, holding the hair dryer up in the flickering candlelight. There was a glass of wine on the counter beside her. She was singing: "Staying Alive."

It took Jo a moment to comprehend the whole picture. When she did, when she had absorbed it, and deciphered it, and understood it, she ran downstairs.

Morley didn't have a clue she had been spotted, didn't have a clue she wasn't still alone.

She turned off the hair dryer. Then she knew. Because as soon as she turned off the hair dryer, she heard their voices, clear as day.

Jordon was first. "I am so bagged," he said. "Let's order in."

Good God! They were home!

"I want to go *out*," said Jo. "It's our last night. I want to take you out."

There was a silence. Morley heard someone's feet on the stairs.

Morley took an involuntary step backwards.

Someone was coming up the stairs.

She clutched her robe around her throat.

The someone coming up the stairs said, "I'm showering first."

It was Jordon.

Morley was cowering in the corner.

That's how he would have found her, cowering in the corner of his bathroom, clutching her robe closed.

But he didn't.

"Jordon," said Joanne. "I'm starving. No shower. Let's go."

And just like that, the footsteps stopped.

Morley heard the sound of Jordon going down the stairs. And the sound of Jordon and Joanne going out.

As soon as she was sure they were gone, Morley began to clean up. She blew out the candles, wiped down the tub, put everything back in her pack.

It was only when she finished that she saw the purse on the bed.

When she saw the purse, she knew what had happened. Someone had been up there. It had to have been Joanne.

Joanne had seen her. Joanne had covered for her. That's why they had gone out to dinner—so she could escape.

Morley slunk back across the street.

"What took so long?" said Dave. "It must be really clean over there."

The flowers came two days later, with a handwritten note.

> *Thanks for looking after the place. The fish is*
> *fine. Plump enough to eat. The place looks great.*
> *We appreciate it. It looks like we are going again*
> *in the spring. Jordon has clients in Rome. Let me*
> *know if we could impose again. There is a sauna*
> *in the basement. I was thinking you might enjoy it.*

Morley will tell this story one day, but not for a while. It is still too close to the bone for that. So far, the only person she has told is Dave. In years to come she *will* tell others, but only after Joanne and Jordon leave the neighbourhood.

When she does, she will say it was outrageous that she got into that bath. "I don't know what I was thinking," she will say.

"But I do know this. I came to like her. She was a good neighbour. Kind. But never more than *that* night. That was one of the kindest things anyone has ever done for me."

SUMMER OF STARS

Aliens. It was aliens. It's happening. They're coming.
—MURPHY

Dave's mother, Margaret, and retired fire chief Smith Gardner, married more than a year, were sitting at the kitchen table. It was lunchtime—canned tomato soup, grilled cheese sandwiches and butterscotch pudding.

They had made it to the pudding when Margaret began the story of Puccini's last opera, *Turandot*—which happens to be her favourite.

The story was part of Margaret's ongoing campaign to educate Smith. Not in the ways of the world—Smith Gardner was already wise in the ways of the world—but in the ways of *her* world.

The campaign wasn't going as well as Margaret would have liked. Smith was a sweet and kind man. She loved having him around her, loved cooking for him. She enjoyed his company. They enjoyed *each other's* company.

Yet there was no denying it. This business of a second marriage—all these little adjustments—was surprisingly tough.

"He didn't finish the final duet," said Margaret.

"Who?" said Smith, putting down his spoon and staring at her, earnestly.

"Puccini," said Margaret, a little peevishly.

"Right," said Smith.

"First he was sick and then he died."

"So he couldn't finish," said Smith, trying to show her that he could keep up.

"So his friend finished it for him," said Margaret.

"Is that allowed?" asked Smith. "It's not against the rules?"

"There are no rules," said Margaret. "This is art, Smith. So his friend finished it. Then the great Toscanini agreed to conduct the world premiere. At La Scala."

Smith raised his spoon as if he were conducting an orchestra. Margaret smiled.

"But when Toscanini reached the last scene," she said, "the scene the friend had written, he put his baton down and turned his back on the orchestra. And everything ground to a halt."

The two of them stared at each other for an uncomfortable moment.

Smith lowered his hands. Smith said, "Why'd he do that?"

"Well," said Margaret, "this is a very famous moment. Toscanini turned to the audience and announced that the maestro had not completed the opera. He said, 'Death is stronger than art.' And *that* would be as far as they would go that night."

Margaret looked exhilarated. Smith looked puzzled.

Smith asked, "Did everyone boo?"

"There was dead silence," said Margaret. "Until someone in the audience yelled out at the top of their lungs."

"I know what he yelled," said Smith. "He yelled, 'I want my money back.'"

"No," said Margaret. "He yelled '*Viva Puccini.*' Then they all stood up. Gave a big ovation."

This made no sense to Smith at all.

"You'd think they would want their money back," said Smith.

Smith had a fiercely pragmatic heart. And Margaret loved him for it. But she wasn't used to it. Her late husband, Charlie, loved the story about Puccini. Loved it. Of course, Charlie loved everything about music. Charlie kept a ukulele in the truck—played it while he drove. He used his knees to steer.

Margaret and Charlie fit together so easily.

Sometimes it felt like there was, it was hard to put this in words … like there was an unanswered question hovering between her and Smith. Like any unresolved question, it kept coming up. It kept demanding attention.

It was there in June, when Margaret told Smith about the opera. And then when her grandson Sam and his best friend Murphy came to spend some of the summer with them, and Margaret had to hustle the boys off each morning before Smith could get to them.

She made the boys sandwiches and pushed them outside to play, before Smith could push them into the garden, and get them pulling weeds or laying down mulch.

"Boys should be *working*," said Smith.

"Boys should be *boys*," said Margaret.

There was no doubt about it, Margaret and Smith were still getting used to one another's ways. But Sam was *her* grandson. So she held trump. And Smith was wise enough not to make her play it. Instead of working, the boys played. Margaret never asked where they had been or what they were up to. It was summer. She *knew* what they were up to. They were up to nothing.

Could anything be more perfect for two boys from the city than to drift around Big Narrows, Cape Breton, in July and August? It was a summer of sweet corn and licorice. Dandelions and frogs. Ice cream and the old wrecked car on the mountain road. And then, *one* night, there were shooting stars.

It was a night Sam and Murphy will never forget. They were in the backyard, lying on the soft grass. The sky couldn't have been blacker. The stars couldn't have been closer—or further away. It was hard to tell. Close and far at the same time. A constellation of confusion.

They had been there for maybe half an hour, lying on their backs, head to head, lost from the world of words, when Murphy said, "Did you see that?"

It was like a flash from a camera, except longer and streakier. It went from one side of the sky all the way across to the other.

The two of them sat up abruptly and stared at each other in wonder.

Whatever it was had flared into the atmosphere of their imaginations like a galloping horse. It was there, and then it was gone. A wave of a hand, a blink of the eye, and they would have missed it. But neither of them had blinked.

"What *was* that?" said Sam.

Murphy's eyes were bulging. But he didn't say anything. It was like he was in a trance.

"Murphy?" said Sam.

"Aliens," whispered Murphy. "It was aliens."

And then there was another. And then another.

And Murphy said, "It's happening. They're coming."

The boys ran inside.

Inside it was an August night like any other. Margaret was sitting on the couch, knitting. Smith was beside her, slouched in his big chair. The television was on. They were watching the news, oblivious that the biggest news of all was just outside.

"We saw a UFO," said Sam.

"Three," said Murphy.

They were hardly the first boys from the city to stare up into the night and be fooled by a shooting star.

"Ah," said Smith, smiling and struggling up.

Margaret knew what was coming. These were the sort of moments Smith loved. He was about to explain. He was about to say something about comets and meteors and cosmic hoo-ha.

"Ah," said Smith. But he didn't get any further. Because Margaret didn't let him. Before Smith said one more word, Margaret shot him a look.

"What?" said Smith. Margaret shot him another look, and then *she* turned to the boys and said, "Tell us what you saw."

"Right across the sky," said Murphy. "Right over town."

"Three of them," said Sam. "One after the other."

"Like a flash from a camera," said Margaret. "Except faster and streakier."

"Exactly," said both boys together.

"How did you know?" said Sam.

"Well," said Margaret, "you're not the first ones around here to see something like that."

She glanced at Smith.

Smith was frowning at her.

Margaret frowned back.

An hour later the boys were upstairs. They were lying in their beds. But they were light-years from sleep.

"Did you see your grandfather?" said Murphy.

"He didn't like her talking about it," said Sam.

"She didn't tell us everything she knew," said Murphy.

"You could tell. Did you see the look she gave him?"

They talked for over an hour, lying on their beds under the sloping roof, feeling smaller and smaller, until they felt like they were floating.

In the living room, Smith turned off the television.

"Why didn't you want me to tell them?" he asked.

Margaret was folding up her knitting.

"What," she said, "that it was just a shooting star?"

"A meteor," said Smith. "Not a star. Probably no bigger than a grain of salt."

Margaret stared at him.

"That's the truth," said Smith.

"Smith," she said. "What sort of fun can a boy have with a grain of salt?"

"But those are the facts," said Smith.

"Smith Gardner," said Margaret, "life would be pretty tedious if all we did was stick to the facts."

Sam couldn't remember falling to sleep. But he slept deep and dreamed of the golden flare from a monstrous spaceship. When he opened his eyes, the first thing he saw was Murphy, already dressed, sitting by the window, staring.

"How long you been up?" asked Sam.

"Maybe they didn't *land*," said Murphy. "Maybe they crashed."

And so they had breakfast, and they busted out the back door and onto their bikes.

"We'll start at Macaulay's," said Murphy.

"Start what?" asked Sam.

"The search," said Murphy.

As they pedalled over the green iron bridge on the edge of town, Sam said, "Why Macaulay's?"

"Because," said Murphy, "Macaulay has the only cows in town. There are almost always mewpilated cows."

Macaulay's cows were fine.

"You're sure?" said Murphy. "All of them?"

They were standing in the farmyard in front of the barn, the boys straddling their bikes, Old Man Macaulay leaning on his tractor.

"I only *have* the one cow," said Old Man Macaulay. "It isn't hard to keep track."

The boys found the piece of spaceship in the woods on Macaulay's Mountain—a piece of shiny metal about the size of a cookie sheet. In fact, if you didn't know better, you might have thought it *was* a cookie sheet. It was half buried under some old leaves not far from Macaulay's sugar shack.

"This could be from a wing," said Sam.

"Or a tail stabilizer," said Murphy.

"It could be radioactive," said Sam.

They collected a soil sample from beside the piece of metal.

They didn't want to touch it, so they used a stick to push it into Murphy's backpack.

They showed the shiny metal to Margaret when they got home.

"Do you think it is radioactive?" asked Margaret.

Smith, who was reading the paper at the kitchen table, snorted derisively.

They thought about selling their find on eBay. But they decided against that. It was too valuable for eBay.

"Besides," said Margaret, "you wouldn't want it falling into the wrong hands."

"Exactly," said Murphy.

Then Margaret looked at Smith and said, "Maybe you should take the boys down to see Chief Kavanagh."

Smith stared at her in amazement. He nodded slightly, as if to say, "I give up."

"You're the lads who found the spaceship," said Chief Kavanagh when they walked into the police station the next morning.

Murphy let out a long contented sigh.

Sam said, "*Piece* of a spaceship."

Chief Kavanagh was sitting at his desk with the morning crossword in front of him. He pushed the paper aside and examined the piece of metal carefully.

"Do you think it is radioactive?" he asked.

He reached for a pen and wrote in his logbook.

It was Chief Kavanagh who suggested they send it to the government.

He sent them to the Big Narrows library. They spent three hours in front of the library's single computer—arguing about where they should send their spaceship part.

To the RCMP? The Space Agency? The Department of Defence? Foreign Affairs?

"What about the Dairy Commission?" said Sam.

Murphy looked up from his book. Murphy said, "What?"

Sam said, "Because of the mewpilated cows."

"How about Tourism?" said Murphy. "They could be tourists."

They narrowed it down to three. Citizenship and Immigration, the Refugee Board and CBDC.

"What's that?" asked Sam.

"Cape Breton Development Corporation," said Murphy, following his finger along the line.

"Perfect," said Sam.

They left with an address written on a tiny scrap of paper.

When they got back to Margaret's, they sat down at the kitchen table to draft a letter. Murphy dictated. Sam wrote.

Murphy said, "Start with this: *We found it in area 27.*"

"Area 27?" said Sam.

"That's the way governments talk," said Murphy.

Murphy began to pace. Sam sat at the table and tried to keep up.

"Wait," said Sam. "Not so fast. How do you spell *mewpilated?*"

"I don't know," said Murphy. "M-e-w ..."

Sam wrote, "There are no dead cows."

Murphy added, "As far as we have seen."

Sam said, "But Macaulay's cow seems cranky."

There are no dead cows, as far as we have seen, but Macaulay's cow seems cranky.

"Good," said Murphy.

They placed the letter and the piece of metal, along with some of the dirt they had dug up, into a cardboard box, and wrapped the box in brown paper. They took the parcel to the post office. They paid for the postage with their own money.

That night after supper, as the boys washed the dishes, they argued about whether gerbils were more fun than hamsters, if sasquatches existed in Canada or just in Russia, and what it would be like if Martians landed and they barked and dogs could understand them but not humans.

When they finished, they went to town to get ice cream. They walked down the hill towards Main Street, as lost in their conversation as two rabbinical students. As he watched them go, Smith felt a pang. His boyhood summers seemed so close and so far away.

When she heard how much the package cost to mail to Ottawa, Margaret wondered if Smith was right. Maybe it was a small treachery not to always tell the truth.

"Maybe I was wrong, Smith," she said one night.

The boys were already in their room, reading.

"Charlie and I ..." she began. Then she started again. "Maybe Charlie and I didn't think these things through enough."

Smith put his hand on Margaret's arm.

"I think *you* have things just about right," he said. "Maybe it is me who doesn't think things through."

"I just enjoy stories," said Margaret, "more than facts. I like the mystery and the tension."

"Ah," said Smith. "That's why you married *me*."

Margaret laughed, but she didn't contradict him. She went into the living room and settled into her chair. She picked up her knitting.

Smith disappeared upstairs. He rooted around at the back of the bedroom closet. He was looking for his old binoculars. When he found them, he crossed the hall and knocked on the boys' bedroom door.

"Come on," he said.

Once he got them downstairs, he handed them the binoculars.

"It's a beautiful night," he said. "Let's not waste it."

They lay down on the lawn, and he lay down beside them. They all looked up. August stars.

Margaret saw them out the kitchen window. Her three boys sprawled on the grass. She made hot chocolate. When she took it out, Sam handed her the binoculars. "Look at the moon," he whispered. "Look at the moon."

Who knows how long they were out there. They stayed until it got cold, until the boys began to shiver. When they had stayed long enough, Margaret took them in. When she came back, Smith was sitting on the porch stairs, still staring at the sky.

She stood beside him for a few minutes, the two of them quiet.

Smith said, "A penny for your thoughts."

"I was just thinking about Charlie," said Margaret. "He would have loved this summer."

"Do you miss him?" asked Smith.

"It seems so long ago," said Margaret. "Another life."

Smith patted the stair beside him and said, "Sit down."

She sat beside him. Smith stood up, took off his cardigan and draped it around her shoulders. When he sat down again, she leaned into him, and they sat there staring at the sky together.

August is a vintage month for boys and a vintage month for shooting stars. You don't have to look long on an August night before you see one. When you do, you can, as the old song says, pick it up and put it in your pocket; or you can make a wish. You can close your eyes and tell yourself that it was *your* wish star that just fell, and you can wish your heart's desire. If you are lucky, your wish will come true, and you will live happily ever after.

Or like Smith and Margaret, on that starry night that August, you can watch it sail across the sky and smile quietly, and know that when stars are falling and little boys are up in their bedrooms reading under sloping roofs, for now, anyway, the world is a safe place. And you can go to bed and sleep long and deep and worry about the rights and the wrongs, the comings and the goings, in the morning.

"There is plenty of time for them to learn that there are no mysteries left in the world," said Margaret.

"There is not close to enough time for that," said Smith. "There are more mysteries than time will ever give us."

Another star flew across the sky.

"How long do you think I'll get?" he said.

"Like a flash from a camera," said Margaret, "except brighter and streakier."

He laughed, and his laugh rose up into the night sky, up to the window where Murphy was sitting. Murphy's book was abandoned upside down on his bed. But the sound of the old man's laughter barely make an impression. Because up in the window, Murphy was also looking at the sky.

"Come here," he whispered to Sam. "Come and see. It's happening, again."

RHODA'S REVENGE

Call the police. And don't make any sudden movements.
—DAVE

It was spring. Each morning seemed to be warmer than the morning before it. The sun shining down, on the trees, on the garden, on the lawn, on all of creation, on every man, woman, child, dog, cat, squirrel, setting every*one* and every*thing* all a-tingling.

It was spring. And the world and everything in it was stretching and shedding, shaking and bursting. The whole kit and caboodle uncurling like a fiddlehead.

It was spring, and for the second sweet day in a row, Morley was spending the day at home—alone.

She had been planning this since February. Three days. By herself. Yesterday she did her office, her bedroom and the hall closet. Tomorrow she was attacking the kitchen cupboards. She wasn't spring *cleaning*. She was weeding. Sorting, packing and throwing out. She was giving her house a haircut.

Today she was in the basement. Morley and Dave have shelves down there. And Morley had taken a cardboard box off the top shelf. Not the first. One of many. That's what she was doing down there—going through things.

Like the other boxes she had sorted through before it, she had set this box on the floor beside her and flipped it open.

It was full of stuff wrapped in tissue—a box of tissue packets.

She had no idea what it was. A vagrant box of Christmas decorations perhaps? Lying on top of all the little tissue packets was a doll.

"What?" said Morley.

She picked the doll up and laid it aside. She picked up the top tissue packet and unwrapped it.

It was her Girl Guide shirt. She held it up. Could she have ever been that small? The second package was an old diary. The third—a packet of letters.

She had, apparently, found a box of keepsakes.

She had a vague memory of putting it away.

Sort of—maybe.

She unwrapped a few more things. The locket her father had given her on her thirteenth birthday. Her first driver's licence.

They all made sense—all these things—except for the doll. She had never seen the doll in her life. She hadn't just *forgotten* the doll. She had absolutely no memory of it—none whatsoever.

"A doll?" she asked, again.

It *was* a little odd.

It's not that Morley didn't have any dolls as a little girl. She had dolls. Most girls have a doll or two. But in her box of keepsakes?

Morley was never what you might call a *girly* girl. She lived on a street with a bunch of boys. And she learned early on that if she was going to get any respect, she wasn't going to get it playing with dolls.

Not that the boys on her street minded playing with her dolls. She had, for instance, a Ken and some Barbies. The boys were always ready to play with *them*. They would, for instance, take Ken and pop off his head and exchange it with Barbie's.

Morley learned to leave her dolls at home when she went out. She learned to be proud of her skinned knees and her messy hair.

Morley's history with dolls was a tale of neglect.

Strangely, her husband, Dave, had his own difficult experience with dolls when he was a boy. I say strangely because in those days, it was not normal for a boy to have much to do with dolls.

But Dave grew up in a small town. And he had a younger sister. So it happened that he grew up with dolls around him, which was not always easy because, when Dave was a boy, dolls terrified him. None more than the doll his sister, Annie, got for Christmas the year of the big spring flood.

It was a life-sized and disturbingly life-*like* baby doll, with a head that flopped around and an earnest but largely vacant expression.

Mostly this doll stared into space, unless you laid her down. When you laid her down, her eyes closed.

Dave thought this was creepy—the way the doll's eyes slid open and shut, and the way they seemed to stare vacantly at you when they were open.

He tried not to show his discomfort, but Annie, with the cruel and unerring sensibility of a sibling, figured it out almost immediately. Sensing a weakness, she set out to exploit it.

The doll was named Rhoda.

"Did you know," Annie said to her brother, one night as they were getting ready for bed, "that when it gets dark, Rhoda comes alive?"

Dave laughed.

"She's a doll. That's impossible," Dave said. "She does not come alive."

Annie saw the flicker of doubt in his eyes. Annie knew she had him.

In fact, he had dreamed of just that, of Rhoda appearing in his room, clutching a knife in her evil little doll hands.

"Yes, she does," said Annie. "And if you are not nice to me, she will get you."

Sure of herself, Annie began to torment him. She brought Rhoda everywhere. She would buckle her into the back seat when they went in the car. She would take her to the park and set her on the swings. Worst of all, she would bring her to dinner. She set a place for Rhoda every night.

Their mother, Margaret, thought this was sweet and played along, until one night when she and Charlie came back from an evening of bridge. It was well past midnight when she went to check on Dave and found him sitting in his room, wide-eyed with terror, clutching a baseball bat.

"Rhoda is going to hunt me down and kill me," he said.

Margaret took one look at her pale son and his dark-smudged eyes and thought, *that boy has not slept in weeks.*

She told him that she would throw the doll out.

Annie was livid. She didn't particularly like Rhoda, but she liked the power Rhoda had conferred upon her. No one was going to throw Rhoda out.

Like any good mother might, Margaret decided that she would try to make both her children happy. She hid Rhoda in the attic crawl space. She told Annie that she had put Rhoda away in a safe place until Dave and Annie could get along. She told Dave she had thrown Rhoda out.

"Did you throw her in the fire?" asked Dave. "You have to burn her."

"Yes," said Margaret. "I burned Rhoda. But don't tell your sister."

Ten years went by.

One spring weekend, Dave, now a teenager, was given the task of cleaning the attic crawl space.

He strapped his uncle's old mining lamp around his forehead and squirmed in through the little door at the back of his parents' closet. He was knee deep in insulation and old Christmas wrapping when his hand landed on the doll's leg. Rhoda rose out of the wrapping paper like she was rising from the dead.

The light of Dave's lamp glinted off Rhoda's plastic forehead. She seemed to be glowing.

And then, to underline her evilness, Rhoda batted her eyes.

Margaret heard Dave's scream all the way downstairs.

"Good heavens," she said, remembering the doll.

She could hear her son tumbling down the stairs.

"Rhoda's alive," he screamed as he flew past her and right through the closed screen door.

Everyone thought it was hilarious. Everyone except Dave. Dave didn't think it was funny at all. Rhoda was returned to Annie's bedroom where she lived on the bookshelf, making occasional surprise appearances in Dave's room—dangling on a rope in his closet on Halloween, tucked into his bed on graduation night.

Dave was already on the road the year he turned twenty-one. He came home for his birthday and his family went out for dinner at the Starlight Room in the Breakwater Hotel. It was just the four of them for dinner, but afterwards some of Dave's friends joined them, and there were presents. The highlight was when Annie gave him Rhoda.

Annie told the whole story, and before she sat down, she made Dave swear that he would never throw Rhoda out.

"Every man needs a woman in his life to keep him in line," she said.

They took a picture of Dave with Rhoda propped in a chair beside him. He refused to hold her.

Dave didn't think it was funny at all.

Of course, isn't it just the way of the world that Dave and Morley, both of them doll impaired, both of them wounded in their own way by dolls, would give birth to a little girl who was besotted with dolls?

Isn't it just the way things work that these two would raise a child who had a room full of dolls?

"There are Barbies and Kens stacked up in there like firewood," said Dave one day. "Where do they come from?"

"I have no idea," said Morley.

Both of them had no clue that their self-reliant daughter had figured out early on that she couldn't count on her parents to help her amass a doll collection and had developed strategies to do it herself. The most successful was a sleepover camp she advertised at school. Stephanie's classmates actually paid for the privilege of sending their dolls to spend four or eight weeks in her bedroom camp, where, Stephanie promised, they would have a multitude of growth opportunities and lots of personal attention. Each doll that enrolled faithfully wrote at least one letter and one postcard home each session.

> *Please let me stay four more weeks. I have made new friends and I am having so much fun. It's such a bargain. I love you.*

By the time she was eight, Stephanie had amassed a collection of such proportions that she had developed a complicated rotation system to manage sleep privileges, ensuring every doll got an equal amount of time in bed with her.

But all that was years ago. And now, all this time later, Morley was sitting on her basement floor, surrounded by tissue, staring at the doll she had pulled out of her box of keepsakes.

The doll perplexed her.

That night as they got ready for bed, Morley looked at Dave and said, "Do you think I am losing my memory? Have you noticed anything?"

It wasn't that she was forgetting where she had put her keys or the name of, you know, the thing that you use to scrape the batter out of the bowl when you are baking a cake. The thing with a wooden handle and a rubber part. That thing.

A spatula.

It wasn't that. She knew she hadn't lost her memory. But she *was* worried that she was losing memories.

More and more of her life seemed to be disappearing into the fog of time. She didn't like *that* one bit.

And so, a little perplexed, a little worried, a little discomfited, Morley did what she often does when faced with a problem she can't solve. She avoided it. She stuck the doll away, in the top of the hall closet.

It stayed there for months.

It stayed there while spring was blown away by the great sigh of summer. And soon enough, it had returned to what seemed like its lot in life. Soon enough, it was, once again, forgotten.

Until a chilly October night. At three in the morning.

It was darker than dark—hours from bedtime and hours from dawn, and Dave couldn't sleep.

He had been staring at the ceiling for hours.

Finally he slipped out of bed and stumbled into the hall.

There was a night light glowing in the bathroom.

By the dull yellow glow of the night light, he opened the hall closet. He was looking for the hot water bottle.

He reached up onto the top shelf.

Later, when she would tell the story, Morley would say the first thing she thought was that her husband had had a heart attack.

Except she always thought heart attacks were silent, slumpy sort of things. Dave sounded more like ...

"Like I was being attacked," said Dave.

When Morley found him, he was lying on the hall floor. On his back.

Rhoda was perched on his chest, blinking.

"Call the police," whispered Dave.

"And don't make any sudden movements."

It was Dave who had put the doll in the box in the basement.

"It's *your* doll?" said Morley.

"I wanted her out of the way," said Dave. "I wanted her out of sight."

None of them, not Morley, not Sam, and not Stephanie, had heard the story about Rhoda.

They have now.

There's a problem with sharing your great weaknesses with your family. Especially if your great weakness happens to be your fear of dolls. The problem is that your family will likely not offer you the level of sympathy or understanding you believe you deserve.

A week passed before Rhoda made her next appearance.

One morning Dave came down for breakfast, and there was Rhoda sitting at the table.

"Ha-ha," said Dave. "Very funny."

A week later she tumbled out of the glove compartment of his car.

The thing about these things is that if they happen enough, they lose their potency. The victim becomes desensitized. The joke loses its punch.

So in a way, the curse becomes the cure.

Dave learned that the morning he opened the microwave and Rhoda tumbled out onto his plate and he felt, instead of fear, a wave of impatience wash over him. He was about to announce this, but checked himself when he spotted Sam peeking from the pantry. Instead of an announcement, Dave clutched his heart and lurched backwards.

His little performance drew Sam out of the pantry. Sam burst into the kitchen, hooting.

He was getting such a kick out of scaring his father that it didn't seem right to break the spell.

Strangely, once he locked into the role of actor, Dave actually became fond of Rhoda, his partner in deception.

But one day over the winter holidays, Stephanie showed up at Dave's shop. She was carrying a bag. She put it down on the counter. It was Rhoda.

"Can you keep her here?" she asked. "At least until I go back to school? She gives me the creeps."

And that's where she is today, sitting on a shelf in Dave's store. By the cash.

If you went in there ever, and you asked Dave about her, he might, if he were in the mood, tell you the whole story, beginning at the beginning. But as likely as not, he will just tell you that it's a doll that used to be his sister's.

FISH HEAD

It wasn't until the next morning that we saw the skull was deformed.
—DAVE

I t was a Saturday, in early May, in Big Narrows. Dave and his son, Sam, were having lunch at the Maple Leaf Restaurant. They were in town for the weekend. They were there to help Margaret with things. It was their spring ritual. Take down the windows. Turn the garden.

Saturday lunch at the Maple Leaf was part of it. Club sandwiches and fries. Vanilla milkshakes.

"Last time," said Sam, "we had grilled cheese."

"We did?" said Dave. "I don't remember that."

Barbara set the shakes in front of then—two tall glasses and an aluminum container with the overflow. She set the overflow down in front of Sam.

"A real shake," said Dave to Sam. "Made with *real* ice cream."

Sam bent his straw down and rolled his eyes.

"It's good," he said. Then he said, "Tell me another. About him."

Dave said, "I don't know. He was a good guy."

It's a hard question. You live your life in minutes and hours. You move along beside the people you love, and in the midst of all the moments, in the middle of all the movement, you don't stop to commit things to memory. You never imagine there is anything that is going to be of historical importance, or that someone is going to come along and quiz you about things.

"But he was my grandfather," said Sam. "And I don't know anything about him."

"I know," said Dave. "I know."

He put his sandwich down. "He liked to play the bass," he said. "His friends would come over to the house on Sunday nights and they would play music."

"I know that stuff," said Sam. "He was slow."

"He wasn't slow," said Dave. "He would fall behind the beat."

Dave was twisting around in the booth. Behind the counter, Barbara held up a bottle of ketchup. Dave nodded.

"Thanks," he said. Then he turned back to Sam.

"Did I ever tell you the one where we jumped off the bridge into the river on our way home from church? I was afraid to jump. Other kids jumped all the time. He wanted to show me I shouldn't be afraid. So he jumped with me."

"In your clothes," said Sam.

"Holding hands," said Dave. "In our Sunday best. He got in trouble for that."

Dave glanced at his son. "You knew that one."

"Yep," said Sam.

He dipped one of his fries into the tiny pot of ketchup Barbara had brought. He ate it, picked up another, and hesitated. Then he looked at his father and said, "How did he die?"

"Heart," said Dave. "He smoked."

"Did it hurt?"

"I don't know," said Dave. "I hope not."

Sam said, "Did I ever meet him?"

Dave said, "He died just before you were born. He would have liked you. A lot."

They finished lunch and walked along to the end of River Street and then took the shortcut along the old railroad tracks up to the High Road. They had just passed the little creek that runs beside the tracks there when Dave said, "Did I ever tell you about the fish head? That's a good story."

Sam shook his head.

"Okay," said Dave. "This is a good one. I had forgotten all about this one."

They still had a way to go, so he told it slow, like a movie.

It began like a movie, anyway. Like a movie about spies. At night, and in a rain so misty it was more like fog.

It was around midnight, in the sneaky month of April. Two shadowy figures scrambling along a riverbank with miners' lamps strapped to their foreheads. The light from the lamps bouncing off the river, and the balsam trees, and the wet rocks along the river's edge.

Here and there, they step over patches of granular, cornlike snow. But mostly the snow is gone from the path, though there is still plenty in the woods, under the trees, where the land is low and bedded with pine needles.

The person in front, the one with the peak hat and the oiled canvas jacket, is carrying two nets. The nets are on long poles, like butterfly nets, but more substantial, made for sturdier things than butterflies.

The second person, the one following, is a boy. He is carrying a rucksack on his back. In the rucksack he has a cheese sandwich, two pieces of black licorice and a homemade sling-shot.

"That's me," said Dave.

The man stops and reaches into his pocket and pulls out a pack of Export A. He shakes a cigarette loose and lights it. When the match is out, he puts it in his pocket beside a mickey of whisky.

"That's my dad. Your grandfather. We're going smelting."

It was the April that Dave was eleven years old. The smelt were running, and everyone knows that the best time to net smelt is in the middle of the night, when the water is ice-cold, and you can use a flashlight to spot the fish in their silvery clouds.

"That was a great winter," said Dave.

It was the first spring he went smelting like that—in the middle of the night, with his dad.

The perfect end to a perfect winter.

It was the night they caught the famous king cod.

Sam said, "How did you catch it?"

Dave picked up a pebble and threw it into the woods.

"I'm not sure," he said.

Sam picked up a pebble and threw it too.

Dave said, "We were never able to explain how we got it. It didn't make any sense."

Neither of them were sure, except to say they had parked the truck at Kerrigan's about eleven-thirty that night and walked down the river past Big Falls. They had stopped and talked to Mr. Macaulay, who was fishing at the bend, near where the logging road crossed, and they had gone maybe a quarter mile further, to where the river narrows by the big rocks. They netted up a good feed of smelt, and just before they left, Charlie somehow ended up with that big Greenland cod in his net.

You see them from time to time in the lake, but no one had heard about one in the river before. That's where they got it, though.

"It wasn't until the next morning that we saw the skull was deformed," said Dave.

He and Charlie were in the shed cleaning smelt when they spotted it. The dog was watching them hopefully from the corner. Fish guts all over the table.

Charlie ran his knife over the bump on the fish's head. He said, "Looks like a crown, see. That's why they call him a *king* cod. Happens from time to time."

Dave said, "What are we going to do with it?"

Charlie said, "We're going to eat him."

Dave meant the head.

Charlie said, "Oh. We'll give the head to the dog."

At the word *dog*, Scout looked up and cocked *his* head hopefully.

When they finished, Charlie gave Dave the gut bucket and told him to empty it behind the shed.

Once he got back there, back where no one could see him, Dave took the king cod head and fetched an old newspaper and wrapped it up. Before he went in for dinner, he took it to the old ice house and buried it in a barrel of pickling salt.

"You still had an ice house?" asked Sam.

"For sentimental reasons," said Dave. "We had a fridge too."

"Why did you keep it?" asked Sam.

"The ice house?" said Dave.

"The fish head," said Sam.

"I don't know," said Dave.

It is hard to remember things like that. He probably didn't even know back then.

Dave shrugged. "I guess I figured having a fish head could come in handy."

Whatever the reason, it was important at the time. And he would check on the fish head every couple of days. He would shimmy over the cool, damp sawdust, reach down into the salt barrel, and pull out the gut-stained newspaper. The cloudy black eyes. The silver skin. The head, which was drying out in the salt and becoming mummified.

He couldn't stop looking at it.

It was there for a month before he told anyone.

"Who did you tell?" asked Sam.

"Billy Mitchell," said Dave.

"Do I know him?"

"No, you don't know him."

It was a Saturday morning. Billy and Dave had pooled their money and gone to MacDonnell's. They got a Lime Rickey out of the cooler and a box of Tom Thumb Potato Chips.

They took the pop and the box of chips to the park by the library. They were sitting on the bench, Billy's bike leaning against one of the big balsams, Dave's lying on the ground. Billy was telling Dave how he was going to see his grandfather in Glace Bay. How he was taking the bus by himself and how his grandfather always took him to the movies.

"He gets me popcorn," said Billy. "And licorice."

Dave said, "What colour?"

Billy said, "Black."

And that's when Dave said, "I have a fish head."

Billy said, "So what?"

Dave said, "It's mummified."

Then he delivered the coup de grâce. "And deformed."

Billy said, "Where is it?"

They parked their bikes behind the ice house.

Dave said, "You wait here." He ducked alone into the sawdust world of ice and closed the ice house door behind him. He didn't want Billy to know exactly where he kept the fish head.

He took in a deep lung-full of the cool damp air and fetched the fish head from the salt barrel. He didn't go right out. He kneeled by the door for a minute. He made himself count it out. Slowly. One cod head. Two cod heads. He wanted Billy to think getting the head was more complicated than it was. There were wet stains and little flecks of sawdust on both his knees when he came out.

They set the head on the ice sled, which was lying in the tall grass beside the ice house.

Sam asked, "Why didn't you want Billy to know where it was?"

Dave said, "Because I didn't want him to come and take it."

It was Billy's idea to boil the meat off.

Billy said, "If we boiled the meat off it, we could see the skull."

They went into the house together. Billy talked to Dave's mother while Dave scooped a handful of wooden matches from over the stove. They got an old apple juice can, and they rode out to the quarry. On the way, they gathered twigs and branches and a handful of birchbark, so they could build a fire.

But when they got to the quarry, Dave decided he didn't want to boil the meat off.

"I liked the way it looked," said Dave. And the way it smelled. The fish head had started to get leathery and to turn a golden colour.

They built the fire anyway.

They poked at it with sticks for a while, and then threw on all the wood to see if they could get the flames as high as their waists.

"Did you?" said Sam.

"I don't remember," said Dave.

They let it burn down, and when it did, they melted things. An old sneaker. A plastic gun. Some webbing from a lawn chair.

"You'd never let *me* do that," said Sam.

And then, their work was done. They let the fire burn down. They peed on it to make sure.

"You peed on it?"

"Yeah," said Dave. "Haven't you ever peed on a fire?"

Sam said, "We don't even have a quarry."

Dave said, "Well, you should try it some time."

Billy came back from Glace Bay and said, "My grandfather has a fish head like yours. He has it hanging in his boathouse. It predicts the weather.

"My grandfather says it talks to him," said Billy.

Dave tied the fish head with some yarn and hung it from a nail at the back of his bedroom closet. He stared at it for days, but it didn't move. And it certainly didn't say anything.

Sam said, "Didn't it smell?"

Dave said, "Maybe a bit. But not like fish. Like the sea."

Then one day, he came home from school, and it had shifted. It wasn't looking the same way.

That night he was woken by the sound of rain on the tin roof. He took his flashlight out of his bedside table and got out of bed. He went to the closet and shone a light on the fish head. The head had spun completely around. It seemed like magic to Dave. It was, in fact, the change in humidity working on the yarn. He went downstairs, the flashlight bouncing off the walls. He opened the side door and stood on the stoop. He held his hand out into the rain to be sure.

When he woke up, the sun was shining and the fish head was back to normal.

He told Billy on the way to school.

"It works," he said.

Billy said, "That's what my grandfather says."

"Anyway," said Dave, "none of that is the important part. The part I wanted to tell you about, the important part, is the day I wore it to school."

"Wait a minute, wait a minute," said Sam. "Did it ever work again? With the rain?"

Dave said, "Over and over. If it was going to rain, it would shift. Always like … twelve hours before."

"All the time?" asked Sam.

"All the time," said Dave.

"What about snow?"

"Just rain."

Sam said, "I can't believe you never told me about this before."

Dave said, "I had forgotten all about it."

Sam said, "How could you forget about this. This is amazing." And he shook his head. Then he said, "Okay. Tell me about wearing it to school."

Dave said, "You are full of questions. Ask me questions."

Sam said, "Okay. How do you wear a fish head?"

"On your belt," said Dave.

"On your belt?" said Sam.

"Well," said Dave, "on your belt loop. Next question."

"Why would you *do* that?"

"That's a good question. I'm not sure. That was a long time ago now. You have to remember, I was nine years old."

"You were eleven," said Sam. "You said you were eleven."

"Yeah, but those were different times. Eleven then was like nine today."

He tied the fish head to his belt loop in the morning before school.

"Like right in front?" asked Sam

"More to the side," said Dave. "Front side."

"You are so weird," said Sam.

"Thank you," said Dave. "Shall I keep going?"

"Yes," said Sam, "tell me."

"So the fish head was tied to my belt loop. With a piece of the yarn."

Dave was in Miss Nicholson's class that year. And his desk was near the door. And that morning he sat at his desk with the fish head tied to his belt just *praying* Miss Nicholson would ask him a question, any question, so he could stand up and answer. Eventually she did.

"What happened?" asked Sam.

"Well, when she noticed the fish head, she sent me to the office, and the principal phoned my dad," said Dave. "Your grandfather."

"I know," said Sam. "Just, what happened?"

Charlie took twenty minutes to get there. He walked into the office and said, "Hello, Ned. What seems to be the problem here?"

Dave was sitting on the chair in the corner of the office, where you sat when you were in trouble, and when his father walked in, the first thing he saw was that Charlie had a fish head tied to *his* belt loop.

"Did your father really do that?" asked Sam.

"Yep," said Dave. "He really did."

"Then what happened?"

"I don't know," said Dave. "He took me home. I think. Or fishing. He might have taken me fishing."

"You don't remember?"

"I do remember he put his hand on my shoulder as we walked out of the office. That made me feel good."

Dave and Sam were coming up to the corner on the last big hill. Almost home.

Neither of them said anything for a while.

As they turned into Margaret's yard, Sam said, "That was a cool thing for him to do. It sounds like he was a good dad."

Dave said, "That's what I said."

Then Dave said, "I think I still have the fish head."

Sam shook his head. Sam said, "So weird."

T hey found the fish head before they went to bed. In a box at the back of Dave's old closet. With a bunch of stuff like that—a little cast-iron cannon, a set of hockey cards, some marbles.

It was leathery and golden, as if it had been smoked. A piece of green yarn was still tied through the top.

Sam was sitting on the bed holding it.

He said, "It doesn't smell. I thought it would smell."

They were both sleeping in Dave's old room. Sam was already in his pyjamas. Dave was getting ready.

Sam said, "Can I have it?"

He was sitting on the bed nearest the window, turning the fish head around in his hands.

Dave said, "I always kind of liked that it was here. If I give it to you, would you leave it here, or take it home?"

Sam said, "I would take it home."

Dave said, "And what would you do with it?"

"I would wear it to school on my belt," said Sam. "Like you."

Dave said, "Why?"

Sam said, "Because. And when *I* have a kid, I will give it to *him* and tell him the story and he will wear it to school. And then it will be a family tradition. I think Grandpa would like that."

Dave laughed. "Yes, I think he would like that very much." And then he turned and stared out the window, his breath fogging the glass.

All these little moments, he thought, *who knows which ones are going to count and which ones will be forgotten.* It's never the things you think. It isn't the fishing trip. Or even the fish. It's the fish *head*.

It's the smoke, never the fire. And the smoke is wily and wispy. The smell of it gets in your hair and your clothes, and no matter how much you try to duck around the flames, the wind always changes. It *always* gets in your eyes.

"What's the matter?" said Sam. "Are you crying?"

"Just a little," said Dave. "But it's okay. It's not unhappy crying. It happens when I come here sometimes. It's like there's a big fire here for me. Sometimes, when I get close to it, the smoke gets in my eyes."

He turned away from the window and sat down on his old bed beside his son.

"Tomorrow we will help Grandma with the garden, and then before supper we will go out to the graveyard, and I will show you your grandfather's grave."

"Can I bring this?" asked Sam.

He was holding the fish head.

ROSEMARY HONEY

Maybe he's dead.
—MURPHY

Just as redemption can only come to those who have lost their way, just as true love only embraces the love-lost, so, too, are dreams handed out. Oh, yes, they come to those who have hitched their wagon to a star, but even stargazers know loss and longing; for before you can dream, you have to long, and before you can long, you have also had to have lost.

For ten years, Dave's neighbour Eugene, now well into his nineties, all spotted and brown with age, has spent his summers sitting in his backyard garden, tipping back precariously in his old kitchen chair, a little cigar in one hand, a tumbler of his famous homemade wine on the table in front of him; and with a dreamer's eye, he has watched over his garden—over the sticky grapes hanging in the shade of the grape arbour, over the languid eggplant and the waxy green peppers, over the fattening red tomatoes and the promise of sweet corn. But more than anything, over the fragrant and silvery bed of rosemary that grows in the sandy soil by his shed.

Sometimes, in the impatient afternoon, he struggles up and makes his way back there. He grabs a stalk of the rosemary, crushes some of the precious needles between his rough fingers and inhales the resinous aroma of lemon and pine. The scent always transports him to the hills of Calabria, back to the dusty little town of Rendi where he grew up—to the farm where the dreaming began.

It has been like this for ten years. For ten years, since he planted them, Eugene has pruned the bushes every fall, covered them for the winter, fed them from the dusty bag of fish meal in the spring and then doted over them in the summer.

Maria, his wife of over seventy years, learned many years ago that if she wants some fresh rosemary for a chicken she is roasting or for bread she is baking, she should not go out with her shears and take it. Eugene has made it clear that the rosemary bushes are not meant for her kitchen, not for her stove, not for her oven and not for the dark bottles of olive oil that line her pantry shelves.

If she needs some, she has to wait until the old fool is napping. Even then, she is careful to snip from the middle of the bush so he won't spot that she has been there.

Eugene sits in his chair and watches over his rosemary patch like an old cat, all sleepy and languid-looking, but watchful all the same. He sits, and watches, and while he watches, he dreams.

This summer, his dream came true.

"Sam!"

It was more a whisper than the command he meant it to be. At ninety, Eugene doesn't so much order as beseech.

"Sam!"

There was barely enough oxygen on this heavy August afternoon to breathe, let alone carry the old man's voice across the yard and over the fence.

Barely audible over the electric buzzing of the cicadas, he called a third time; and this time, Dave's son Sam, roused from the torpor of his own summer dreams, looked up and saw the old man waving at him impatiently. *Come here.*

Last summer, Sam would have *walked* around—out his yard and across the driveway. But this summer, long of leg and coltish of mind, he vaulted over the fence—pleased with the grace of his jump.

"Sam," said the old man.

Eugene was too caught up in *his* dreams to be impressed by the flight of boy over fence.

He waved his cigar so close to Sam's face that the smoke stung the boy's eyes.

"Sam," said Eugene, pointing. "What do you see?"

He was staring at Sam with pre-emptive indignation—as if the boy was about to tell him there was *nothing* to see. That he was *imagining* things.

Sam followed his gaze to the back of the garden.

"Flowers?" asked Sam, uncertain of what it was he was supposed to notice.

"What else?" said Eugene. He sounded urgent, now. Almost frantic.

Sam had never seen him like this.

"The shed?" said Sam, peering back there, puzzled.

"No. No. No." said Eugene. "The flowers. The flowers. What else—about the flowers?"

"They're blue," said Sam. "And white."

The old man was shaking his head. Not that. Not that. Not the *colour* of the flowers.

"I don't know what you are asking me," said Sam.

"What else do you see?" asked Eugene. "*In* the rosemary. What do you see *in* my rosemary bushes?"

"Bees?" said Sam, uncertainly. "There are bees in the rosemary."

"Bees!" said Eugene. And he slumped into his chair, his eyes closing. Exhausted.

"*Honey* bees," he whispered.

This was the moment he had been waiting for. *This* is what he had been dreaming about.

Rosemary honey.

The old man's eyes were still closed. He was breathing fast.

"Mr. Conte?" said Sam, suddenly afraid. "Mr. Conte? Are you all right?"

It was so long ago. So long ago now the memory was like a black-and-white movie—all flickering and faded in his mind. His grandfather. The path up the sun-soaked hill. The hot summer wind. The tree with the strange carvings—marks his great-great-grandfather had cut into the trunk. Marks that claimed the tree, and its honey, for their family.

He thought of them often, those days. The buzzing of the bees, the puffing of the smoke pot, clouds of smoke under the cloudy blue sky, all cloudy in his memory.

He is thinking of his grandmother now. She is in her kitchen. She is wearing her black apron and dress. There is the yeasty smell of homemade bread, the salty tang of fresh goat cheese, and on the rough kitchen table, the very table he had in his own kitchen today, the famous jar of honey. *Rosemary* honey. In all his life, nothing had ever tasted so clean, so fragrant, so flowerlike.

"**M**r. Conte?"

The old man opened his watery eyes. He looked up at the boy. He said, "I need your help."

It was not the first time he had asked. For years, on Sunday nights, Sam has taken his computer over to Eugene and Maria's. He opens emails from their son, Tony, and reads them aloud. He types and sends their replies. Sometimes he runs errands, goes to Mr. Harmon, the grocer, for them, or to Lawlor's Drugstore.

But this was different.

The old man was holding his arms out. He had never done that before. Sam bent down. Eugene grabbed onto him and pulled himself roughly up and out of his chair.

They walked to the end of the garden and stood in front of the rosemary patch.

The old man pointed at the bees.

"Follow them," he whispered. "Find out where they go."

How do you follow a bee?

How do you follow a bee on a beeline?

"To follow a bee," said Eugene "you must think like a bee."

"How do you think like a bee?" asked Sam.

"Eugene!" It was Maria.

"I will tell you tomorrow," he said. "Now go." And he waved his hand in the air dismissively.

He hated all this. This growing old. His old legs aching, even in the sun.

It was the following afternoon.

He was watching Sam and that other boy over the fence. They were huddled over something. They were oblivious to him.

He didn't like asking for their help. He liked it better when *he* helped *them*. Last summer, or was it the summer before? Who could remember these things? He had helped them build the waterslide. He had slid down it himself—from the second-floor bathroom window all the way to the garden. He wouldn't do that now. That was crazy. He could have killed himself.

Sam was supposed to come back. He had clearly forgotten.

And so Eugene sat there tilting back on his chair, watching them. He fell asleep dreaming of water. When he woke, Sam and the other boy were standing in front of him. He didn't have to open his eyes. He could *feel* them staring. He *knew*.

They were whispering. They were saying something about him.

"Maybe he's dead," said Murphy.

Murphy has always wanted to see a dead person.

"He's asleep," said Sam. "You can see him breathing. We should go."

Don't go, thought Eugene.

"If we wake him," said Sam, "we might scare him. He might fall."

Right. He was still tilting—perfectly balanced on the two back legs of his chair, floating halfway between the table and the fence. He wasn't sure how he did it. Practice maybe. God knows, he had enough. But even he was impressed that he could do it in his sleep. His legs unconsciously calibrating the air. As if he were a bird riding a thermal.

"If we scare him," said Sam, "he could go over backwards."

Go on, scare me, thought Eugene.

Maybe I should scare them, thought Eugene. *Go over backwards, see what happens.* Instead he tipped forward and landed with a thump.

They both jumped.

"I'm awake," he said.

He stared at Sam. Then he raised his hand and pointed at Murphy.

"I told you not to tell anyone," said Eugene.

Sam said, "This is my friend Murphy, Mr. Conte. You have met him before. We can trust him. He is going to help us."

Murphy nodded.

Eugene looked Murphy up and down.

Murphy took off his glasses and wiped them on his shirt.

"Sit down," said Eugene.

Both boys sat down at the table.

It turns out, following a bee is not a complicated business.

"It is very simple," said Eugene. "I have done it myself. In the old country."

They would take a plate.

"Like this one," said Eugene, holding up the plate in front of him.

They would cover it with honey.

Eugene picked up the spoon and dipped it in a jar of honey Maria had brought him. He held it over the plate.

"Not too much," he said. "Just enough."

Then they would set the plate with the honey on the ground by his rosemary patch.

"And this is the important part. You have to watch it. Carefully." When Eugene said this, his right eyebrow crawled high on his forehead. Like a caterpillar.

Both boys nodded.

"The bees will come to the plate. And fill up. When they are full, they will fly back to their hive."

The boys would sit and watch them. And move the plate along the line they were travelling. The beeline. Like pawns on a chessboard, they would follow the bees back to their hive one square at a time.

"I would do it myself if my legs weren't so old," said Eugene.

Then he reached into his pocket and pulled out his package of miniature cigars.

"Smoke?" he said, flipping it open and holding it out.

Both boys shook their heads.

Eugene shrugged. He was trying to thank them. They didn't seem to care.

"These things aren't easy to come by," he said.

It took them five days to find the hive. They started the next morning. Every day inching their plate of honey through the neighbourhood. Down the street past the Turlingtons', along the alley behind Lawlor's. It made them feel important. Even better, it made them feel old.

They each took a book with them. They pretended to read when people walked by them. They were, after all, sworn to secrecy.

One afternoon the bees, which had been flying *away* from them, were suddenly flying *towards* them.

"We've overshot," said Murphy. "We've gone too far."

They backtracked.

The hive was in a tree on the edge of the park. There was a hole in the tree as round as a baseball. There were bees everywhere, circling the tree with the certainty of summer.

"That's it," said Murphy.

"We found it," said Sam.

"In a tree," said Murphy.

"In the park," said Sam.

Eugene smiled. He didn't think they had the patience. "You're sure it is the right one? These ones." He gestured towards the rosemary.

"We followed them," said Sam.

"We're sure," said Murphy.

"Take me to the shed," said Eugene.

They helped him up, and they walked beside him, to the back of the garden and into the cool, moist garden shed. He stood by the door and told them what to do. They pulled wooden crates off the shelves. They pawed through them until they found what he was looking for.

It looked like a lantern with a spout. His great-grandfather's smoker.

Eugene sent the boys to gather twigs. He got them to soak pine needles in water. He taught them how to light the smoker. Once it was going, he told them they were going to pretend the doorknob on the shed was the hole to the hive.

"Back and forth, back and forth," he said as they snuck up on the shed, smoke pouring out the smoker's spout. "Slowly, slowly," he said.

"Slower," he said, "like the priest with the thurible."

They both stopped and looked at him.

"Like *what*?" they said.

"Never mind," he said. "Never mind. Just go slowly. Don't excite them. Slower. Let the smoke do the work. It puts them to sleep. Not yet. Not yet.

"Now!

"Now reach in, not so fast. You don't want to make them mad. Slower than that. Okay. You're in. You feel for the honeycomb. You take … just a bit. The top layer. You take yours, you leave them theirs. Half and half. That's fair. It's important to be fair, always. Especially with bees."

Eugene was afraid he was asking too much of the boys. If they made a mistake, if they went too fast, if they used too little smoke, if they panicked—if, if, if—if one of a thousand things went wrong, if the bees sensed their fear. He had seen what could happen when you made a mistake. He had seen bees on the attack, seen them flying in, like little Messerschmitts. A bee sting is no joking matter. It is like having your finger slammed with a hammer. And when you are fighting bees, there can be too many fingers, too many hammers.

Why weren't they back? They had been gone over an hour. Surely it shouldn't take them an hour.

It took two. Fifteen minutes to get the honey and an hour and three-quarters to get their nerve. They stared, and studied, and they considered, for an hour and three-quarters. Then they moved in.

They decided Murphy would work the smoker and Sam would stick his hands in the tree.

"He's your neighbour," said Murphy.

It went off without a hitch. And now they were back. They were standing in front of Eugene. All three of them staring at the oozing piece of honeycomb lying on the newspaper on the picnic table. It was the size of a slab of cheese.

"Do we have to wash it or something?" asked Murphy.

Beside the honey, there was a bottle of Eugene's homemade wine. And beside the wine, three glasses.

Eugene picked up the bottle and opened it with great ceremony. It was from seven summers ago. His best year.

He poured out three glasses of the dusty brick-coloured burgundy. Then he picked up his glass and held it in the air in front of the boys.

"Grazie," he said.

Murphy picked up his glass and held it up in the air, cleared his throat, stared directly at Eugene and said:

"Cento di questi giorni." You should live for one hundred years.

Sam looked at Murphy and whispered, "Where did *that* come from?"

"Goodfellas," said Murphy.

And the two of them dumped their wine on the ground.

As if she had been waiting for a cue, Maria Conte came out the basement door carrying a large wooden tray. There was cheese on it, a bowl of coarse sea salt, a loaf of homemade bread and a dark-green bottle of olive oil.

"Mange," she said. *"Mange."*

Eugene put his hand in the air. Not yet.

He reached into his suit jacket pocket and fumbled around.

He pulled out a set of false teeth. He held them over his head and waved them around with a little flourish.

Sam nodded earnestly.

Murphy said, "*Bene.*"

Eugene opened his mouth and worked the teeth in place. He smiled a toothy smile. He picked up the honeycomb and broke off three small squares. He laid them on the table in front of him. Then he picked one up and brought it to his nose and inhaled. The aroma made him smile. He held it out in front of him and stared at it again. Finally, he stuck it in his mouth. He sat back and chewed.

Everyone was watching him. No one said a word.

He chewed and he chewed.

And they waited.

And slowly, slowly, ever so slowly, he began to grin.

A hive of bees is like a harvest kitchen. They gather up the summer, the heat of the sun, the warmth of the rain, the softness of the mornings and the long afternoons. Above all, they gather up the flavours of flowers—they gather it all up and cork it in wax.

"*Bene,*" said Eugene. "*Bene, bene, bene.*"

There was a tear running down his cheek.

It was like he remembered. It was the warm and waxy stuff of his childhood. He closed his eyes so he could concentrate. Letting it roll over his mouth like a good wine. The sweetness on his tongue, the bitterness at the back of his throat.

He waved his hands over the table and looked at the boys like a priest saying the benediction. Then he nodded, and Sam and Murphy tore off pieces of the bread and dipped them in the bowl of green olive oil. They spread the bread with the cheese. They sprinkled the cheese with salt, and finally, they drizzled it all with honey.

They had never tasted honey sweeter or stronger. It made them both cough.

When they were finished, Eugene said, "I should have gone with you."

"We did it exactly the way you showed us," said Sam.

"You did a *good* job," said the old man. "I wish I went with you. I should have gone."

Sam looked at Eugene for a moment, and then he stood up and said, "We'll be back in a minute."

"Come on," he said to Murphy.

They were longer than a minute. When they came back, they were pulling Sam's old wagon.

They helped Eugene get in it and off they set.

They followed the beeline that they had tracked all week. Or they followed it as best they could. And as they did, they showed him the way it had been.

"They come over that fence," they said. "Through those trees."

Eugene sat in the wagon holding the sides tightly, all shrunken and hunched over. Each time he saw someone walking towards them, he straightened up, staring ahead as they passed, daring them to say something.

They stopped five yards from the tree.

They stood there and stared.

After a few moments, Eugene began fussing with his coat. He was looking for something. When he found it, he held it out and smiled at the two boys. A leather-sheathed knife.

It had once belonged to his grandfather.

He held his arms out, the same way he had held them out a week ago, when he had called Sam and Sam had vaulted over the fence.

He said, "I want to mark this tree with my family mark. So everyone will know it is our tree. Our honey."

Sam wasn't sure you could do that in a park. But he helped Eugene up. He helped him up and over to the tree.

When he got there, Eugene leaned against the trunk, but he couldn't manage the knife. He tried, but he wasn't strong enough. He held onto the tree for a moment, breathing fast. The boys waited.

He handed Sam the knife.

"You do it," he said.

Sam took the knife and said, "I don't know how to make the Conte mark."

Eugene shook his head. "No Conte mark," he said. "Your mark, Sam. This tree is your tree."

Last summer Sam would have been scared to cut into the tree, unsure of what you were allowed to do to a tree in a park. A few years from now he would not have been round for the old man to call. But this summer he *was* around and he was the perfect age for the command. And so while Eugene waved the smoke machine, Sam, and then Murphy, carved their initials six inches above the entrance to the hive.

They are not perfect—Sam's *S* looks like an 8, but you can tell what it is if you are foolhardy enough to get close.

T he bees will live in that tree for many years yet.

The boys will never take honey again.

But Sam will come back every year and look at the mark, even after the bees have left. And he will remember this moment always, this moment standing by the tree, holding the knife. He will remember the moment and he will remember the moment in Eugene's backyard, eating the honey, and how it was both sweet and bitter. And how he and Murphy spent a week that summer on the trail of bees.

He will also remember what Eugene said in the backyard. He said it again when they were leaving the park. It was a simple thing, but it seemed to Sam, even back then when he was still a boy, to carry more weight than the old man meant.

"It is important to be fair always," Eugene said as they left the park, "but it is especially important with bees."

THE HAUNTED HOUSE OF CUPCAKES

I think he is kidnapping him. We should get out of here.
—BECKY

Of all the holidays that mark the slow pendulum swing of the year, of all the smoky days of atonement and thanksgiving, of confession and continuity, of all the summonses that sound in the hearts of the sinners and the saints, of the faithful and the faith*less*, none of them, not Christmas nor Ramadan, Yom Kippur nor Easter, resonate more in the souls of the innocent—which is to say, in the souls of children—than the summons that is sounded at the end of every summer, on All Saints' Eve.

All *Hallows'* Eve.

Let me state the case for Halloween.

It has been, since *I* was a boy, was before that, and is still today, a glorious day to be a child. Maybe the best of days. In its secular certainty, in its wicked and windy way, it *might be* one of the best days we will ever know.

Long unencumbered by the weight of religion, it beckons both the believer and the non-believer into the church of gluttony, into the scriptures of trick-or-treat—into the holy land of sugar.

Like all holy quests, however, it is not an easy road. On Halloween a child is required to leave safe things behind her;

to trade the comfort of day for the chaos of night; to enter a world where candles flicker, leaves blow, hobgoblins scurry and children … must be brave.

A world where memory rules—and memories are made.

Ask Dave, for instance. If you were to take Dave and put him in a witness box, and make him swear to tell *the truth, the whole truth and nothing but the truth so help him God,* and duly sworn, ask him which of all the holidays he recalls from his boyhood, there would be no question, no question at all. It would be—*nolo contendere*—Halloween.

And of all the Halloweens, of *all* the pumpkins in *all* of his life, the one he remembers best … is his first Halloween ever.

He is remembering it at the dining-room table. His daughter, Stephanie, has come home for the weekend with her boyfriend, Tommy. It is Saturday night. Dinner is over. But no one has left the table. And he's well into it.

Kindergarten, Big Narrows Elementary. In the town of Big Narrows, Cape Breton, Nova Scotia. It could have been yesterday.

The school hallway transformed into a magical and bewitching place—black construction-paper witches with stuck-on autumn leaves, the most fantastic art he has ever seen. The exquisite, and almost unbearable, month-long buildup; and then, the night itself—the school's Halloween party. The delicate terror of going to school after dark. Everyone was handed a bottle of pop at the door, which they dumped into a big soup pot to make a witches' brew.

"Cool," said Sam.

"Oh, it was *very* cool," said Dave. "We were taken to the lunchroom."

They sat on the floor, the entire citizenry, and they watched the teachers, who were on the stage, behind the backlit white sheet, all of them dressed as surgeons.

And what were they doing? They were pulling a string of sausages out of the principal's belly.

After *that*, the students were led, one by one, to the basement—into the terrifying haunted house that the grade sevens had built down there. Down the janitor's stairs they went, through the boiler room, along the narrow passage behind the furnace, past the flaking concrete foundation and all the spiderwebs, into the janitor's lunchroom. Where they were blindfolded.

Sightless, they stuck their hands into the pot of teachers' brains, the bowl of stomach guts and the jar of eyeballs.

After that, they were led to the janitor's desk, which was lit by a single candle. There they were shown the fossilized cat that Stephen Kerrigan's father had found in the grocery store wall when they expanded the butcher shop.

"That's the Halloween *I* remember," said Dave. "Hands down."

Of all his yesterdays and todays, that trip to the basement stands out more than any Easter dinner, Thanksgiving supper or Christmas morning. So help him God.

But there have been others.

Morley would tell you about the disasters.

"Tell one," said Sam.

"Well, for instance, the year your father waited until the last minute to get a pumpkin. And when he finally went out, every place he went to was *sold out*."

Sam turned to Tommy and said, "He came home with a watermelon."

"And he spray-painted the watermelon orange," said Morley.

And then he sat at the kitchen table and carved it.

Disaster averted.

"That wasn't even close to a disaster," said Dave. "That wasn't even desperation. That was quick thinking. That's what that was.

"If it's *disaster* you want," said Dave, "let me tell you about the Halloween I was ten."

That would be the October when ten-year-old Dave happened upon the stash of candy his parents had bought weeks in advance of Halloween.

At the beginning of that October, Dave's parents, Charlie and Margaret, had been swept up in an uncharacteristic spasm of organization—who knows how these things happen. Recognizing the danger of what they had done, Margaret hid the candy in the woodshed cabinet.

She was hiding it from her husband as much as from her son. But it was her son who found it. The crime started out innocently—with just one miniature Crispy Crunch.

Can you blame him for that?

And it was followed by ... *just one more.*

And then, God help him—*who among us would throw the first stone?*—one more after that.

By the weekend, he had eaten everything.

"Everything?" asked Tommy.

"Every last piece," said Dave.

"He ate it *all*," said Sam, looking at Tommy.

Too afraid to say anything, Dave left the empty paper bag for his mother to find. Which she did. On Halloween night. When she did, she summoned Dave into the kitchen—the courthouse of domestic discipline—where he was summarily tried, convicted and sentenced.

His punishment? He was sent out with a pillowcase to collect candy around the neighbourhood and told to bring it home immediately so Margaret had something to hand out.

"You want to talk disasters," said Dave, shaking his head.

But that wasn't the half of it.

For that Halloween, the Halloween Dave was ten, the Halloween he ate his parents' stash and had to hand over all his candy in retribution, was the Halloween Dave's sister Annie came home and dumped her bag of loot theatrically onto the living-room floor—a full pillowcase of chocolate bars and chips, licorice and popcorn.

"She was *ankle-deep* in candy," said Dave. "And then she sat down in the middle of it and organized it. Into piles."

When she had finished that, she went upstairs and got a pad of graph paper. She counted out how much she had in each pile. And as she counted, she shaded in the boxes on her graph.

At the end of the night, she had an exact count of everything.

"She rationed it out," said Dave, "so it lasted 365 days."

As the months wore on, Annie's treasure trove became increasingly stale, but that was a minor annoyance, easily outweighed by her pride and the intense sense of satisfaction she got eating her daily ration—under her brother's nose.

"Don't even think of stealing any," said Annie, waving her clipboard at him. "I know *exactly* what I have here."

She *did* share some of it. Before she had lugged her treasure upstairs that Halloween night, to hide it in her room, she had done one last thing.

She had meticulously removed all the items she considered undesirable—the apples, the boxes of raisins, those disgusting molasses kisses. She had put *them* into a separate bag, which, in a magnanimous gesture of faux-generosity, she allowed Dave to pick from. She salted the bag with just enough real candy to keep him coming back. She made him pick in front of their parents—demonstrating to the entire family that she understood what it meant to share.

"You want to talk about a disaster," said Dave. "*That* was a disaster."

"**W**hat about you, Mom?" asked Sam.

"Where do I begin?" said Morley.

Strangely, the world of dress-up has bedevilled Morley all her life. I say *strangely* because she does, after all, work in theatre.

You might think she would be good at this.

"I'm not," said Morley. "I am horrible at costumes."

And she's right. She *is* horrible.

Nevertheless, when Stephanie was old enough to go out, Morley decided it was her motherly duty to make her daughter's costumes.

Steph would begin talking about them in April.

"I want to be a—unicorn Pegasus."

"I want to be a—ballerina hippopotamus."

"I want to be a—101 Dalmatians."

The costume was always a moving target. In the spring, it changed by the week; in the fall, by the day. In October, it could change by the hour. The art of hitting a bull's eye had less to do with aim than with knowing when to pull the trigger.

The year Steph was five, 101 Dalmatians seemed to be, if not close to the centre, at least close to the target.

Morley waited until the Monday before Halloween before she committed. That afternoon she went to a sewing store and sorted through piles of patterns and fabric. It took three days to finish the costume. But when she was done, she was sure she had made an awesome Dalmatian costume.

"It *was* awesome," said Morley.

Maybe.

But on Halloween night, when they got to the first house, and the neighbour—who will remain nameless—opened her front door, she stared at Stephanie, who was standing there in all her Dalmatian splendour, and she blurted, "Wow! What a great cow costume!"

Stephanie burst into tears and cried the rest of the night. Talk about disasters.

But these are the moments you remember.

"Tell the next year," said Sam.

"It wasn't the next year," said Morley. "It was the year after the next year."

"The year I was Batman," said Stephanie to Tommy.

"And I was Robin," said Sam.

It was the last time Morley made their costumes.

"That's for sure," said Morley.

Sure enough, the very same neighbour was peering at them

again. "Let's see," said the neighbour, standing on her stoop, smiling.

"Batman and Robin," mouthed Morley desperately at her neighbour, over her children's heads.

"Batman," mouthed Morley, pointing at Stephanie.

"Robin," she mouthed, resting her hand on Sam's shoulder.

"Let's see," said the neighbour, nodding triumphantly.

"You!" she said, smiling at Stephanie, "are a rat!

"And you!" she said, turning to Sam, "you must be the exterminator."

Sam's friend Murphy made their costumes the following year.

"No, he didn't," said Sam.

"I thought he did," said Dave.

Dave was confused. He was thinking of the famous double-costume grift. Murphy didn't make the costumes. But the sting was Murphy's idea.

"It was brilliant," said Sam.

Here's how it worked.

Murphy and Sam each went out early, and they each worked the neighbourhood solo. After an hour, they went back home, emptied their bags. Then they met in the schoolyard, switched costumes and went back and made another pass.

It was double-dipping, no doubt about it.

"More like reloading," said Sam. "It was awesome."

Most awesome of all, it went off without a hitch.

Over the years, they learned the later they went, the more candy they got.

"That's right," said Sam, nodding his head, earnestly. "At the beginning of the night, people are afraid they are going to run out. Later, they just want to get rid of it."

Stephanie developed her own traditions over the years. Most of them were defensive. On Halloween night, for instance, after she'd returned from her rounds, Stephanie would sit cross-legged in the middle of her pile, in the middle of the living room, and she would unwrap each item she had collected, lick it, and then re-wrap it. It was a strategy designed to keep her brother away from her stuff. It took several hours, but when she was done, no one wanted to go near her stash, let alone eat it.

Last year at this time, Dave confessed that it was him, and not Sam, who had been pilfering her candy over the years.

"It was for your own good," he said.

But of all the Octobers, of all those years, there is one that stands out above the others.

"Tell that one," said Sam, looking at his sister.

It was the first Halloween Stephanie went out alone.

"Tell it," said Sam.

"I went as a crayon," said Stephanie.

"The year before," said Sam, "she went as a pea."

"A green pea," said Dave.

She wore a green cloth body rounded out with chicken wire, green tights, a green leafy headdress and green face paint.

"Mommy," said Stephanie, when she saw her costume for the first time. "It is perfect."

That's because Morley didn't make it.

Instead of making it herself, Morley had enlisted the help of a seamstress she knew.

And though it might have been great, it *wasn't* perfect.

There is not a lot of turning room on a front porch when you are wearing a large, wire-reinforced, green body. Stephanie spent that Halloween, the year she was a green pea, wiping out little pink princesses and fairies with every turn. She left a trail of scattered candy and whimpering kids behind her.

The next year, the first year she went out by herself, the year she is telling them about, all she wanted was to be tall and thin.

She made her own costume that year—out of poster boards.

"I am a crayon," she said, when she came downstairs.

But she had miscalculated. She was such a tall crayon she couldn't fit under porch roofs. She had to crawl up to half the houses she visited.

And if *that* wasn't bad enough, more than one father asked her if she was a stovepipe.

"It was the first Halloween I went by myself," said Stephanie.

"You went with Becky," said Sam.

"Without a *parent*," said Stephanie.

They had been out for an hour when they began to hear the rumours about the cupcake house.

It was a brick house, with a big wraparound porch, in the next neighbourhood. They were giving away cupcakes with buttercream icing and crushed Smarties.

Then they heard there was money baked into the batter. Then someone said you got a can of pop with your cupcake.

"We have to find it," said Stephanie.

"We aren't supposed to leave the neighbourhood," said Becky.

They hadn't actually *seen* anyone with a cupcake. But other kids had. Or said they had. Everyone was talking about it. Everyone had heard something.

Where *exactly* they had to go wasn't exactly clear. Becky and Stephanie set off nevertheless.

They crossed the street at the traffic light near the shoe store and walked into the next neighbourhood.

The houses were bigger there, and farther apart. And the streets felt darker. And the children seemed older.

They walked for a block, and then another.

Becky said, "I don't like this. I have a feeling something bad is going to happen."

Up ahead, a group of teenagers were bumping down the sidewalk.

Stephanie said, "Hold your bag tightly. Keep it close to your body."

Becky said, "I think we should go back."

The teenagers blew by them like a chilly wind.

They didn't go back. They kept walking. For half an hour. More. Until it was getting late.

Becky reached into her bag and pulled out a pack of licorice. She said, "I am a little afraid."

A man walked out of the darkness towards them. He was holding a small boy to his chest. The boy was screaming, and squirming, and kicking his feet.

"I think he is kidnapping him," said Becky, unwrapping a chocolate bar. "We should get out of here."

A front door opened. Across the street another man leaned over the pumpkin on his stoop. He removed the lid and blew out the candle inside it. He stepped back into his house, and the porch light snapped off. The blue smoke from the candle curled into the darkness.

Becky said, "I think we should go back now."

Stephanie said, "We are not going back."

Stephanie kept walking.

Truth be told, she would have gone back, but she wasn't exactly sure where they were anymore.

She wasn't sure *how* to go back.

And that's when she saw it—the big house with the wraparound porch.

"This is it," said Stephanie.

"It doesn't have a pumpkin," said Becky. "Or anything."

But the porch light was on. And Stephanie was already heading up the walk.

Becky was standing beside her on the porch when the old woman answered the door.

The woman was wearing an apron. She was thin and stooped.

She had a bowl of hard candies on a chair by the door. She held out the bowl and said, "Help yourself."

As Stephanie choose a candy, the old woman said, "Take more."

Then she said, "Would you like to come in for a moment?"

Becky gasped.

"Would you like a hot chocolate?"

Becky stepped back.

But Stephanie said yes and dropped to all fours.

She was crawling through the door.

Becky wasn't about to stay on the porch by herself, so Becky went in too.

The lady poured milk into a saucepan. She said that she wanted to get to know the children in the neighbourhood. She said she had decided that tonight was the best night of the year to do it.

"But you are the first ones who have come in," she said.

The lady's name was Mrs. Gibson.

They stayed about fifteen minutes. And then they left.

"That's so crazy," said Sam. "I wouldn't have gone in. Not for a million bucks."

"I had a feeling," said Stephanie. "I could tell."

This happened the Halloween Stephanie was twelve.

In the years since, Stephanie has seen Mrs. Gibson from time to time. Once in Dorothy Woodsworth's bookstore, once in the library and a couple of times on the street. When they see each other, they always say hello.

Stephanie and Becky never got their cupcake. But Stephanie has always felt they did something good that night, something worthwhile, by going in.

It is the Halloween *she* remembers. She always will.

A dark night, leaves swirling in the street, the moon rising behind the bare limbs of the trees. Stephanie crossed the street at the shoe store and stepped into a world of mystery and wonder, and she was never the same. When she came home, something had shifted.

On a night made for children, she left her childhood behind.

MIDNIGHT IN THE GARDEN OF ENVY

You understand the goldfish was dead, right?
—DAVE

July landed on the city like a life ring. Through April, and May, and then unbelievably, all the way through June, the days were wet, miserable and grey. It was the coldest spring anyone could remember.

And then came July. The kids got out of school, and someone turned on the furnace. Overnight, it got hot.

August was even worse. By August, stepping outside was like stepping *into* the furnace. It was hot when you went to bed and hotter still when you woke up.

So maybe we shouldn't be surprised that August was the month that everyone lost it.

When I say everyone, I mean certain people in Dave's neighbourhood.

August was the month when this neighbourhood of nice people who generally get along turned against each other.

It's a dubious science that tries to pin down the origins of anything. The closer you get to the starting line, the murkier things *always* get. But if you wanted to dig into the hot muck of Dave's summer—a summer that started benignly enough, then took a bad turn—one place to begin would be the previous June, the afternoon when Mary Turlington, seized by some earthy spasm, turned *her* attention to her back garden. Who knows where the spark came from that ignited Mary. Probably she saw something in some magazine. Or on one of those television shows. Anyway, there was a spark, and Mary got going.

By going, I don't mean that she and Bert spent an afternoon at Harmon's, loading the trunk with flats of geraniums. We are talking about the summer of the pea-stone pathway, the teak gazebo, the Japanese azalea and, above all, the granite terrace set in Italian clay. Expensive? Not just anyone can lay a terrace like that. You have to have craftsmen experienced in these things.

There is nothing like a neighbour throwing money around their garden to make you feel bad about yours.

Morley had always enjoyed her backyard: the pear tree with the picnic table under it—the scene of so many happy summer evenings—and the little bed of flowers by the garage.

Suddenly her yard seemed diminished. Shabby.

She took a stab at it herself that summer. *She* went to Harmon's and got the geraniums. But next to the gazebo and the terrace, she didn't stand a chance.

The following winter Morley and Dave went to Mexico. Just a week. Dave's old pal Dunkin' Donald Duclos finally convinced them to come down to his place in Yucatan. They ate avocados right from the front yard. In the afternoon, they read in Donald's walled garden, surrounded by all the little coloured birds.

"This is heaven," said Morley. "I love this."

Every night they fixed dinner using herbs from the garden by the door.

"What is this stuff?" she asked one night as she brought a basket of green leaves into the kitchen.

"Ahh," said Donald. "Mexican climbing mint. The king of herbs."

Morley was rubbing a leaf between her fingers. "I get mint," she said, inhaling. "But I also get lime."

"And rum," said Donald. "There is a distant aroma of rum."

"A garden full of mojitos," said Dave, raising his head off the couch.

Dave brought a little cutting home at the bottom of his suitcase. Donald wrapped it in a red bandana he claimed had once belonged to Willie Nelson. When Dave got back, he hid it in the basement freezer. He didn't tell Morley. He wanted to surprise her.

It wasn't a gazebo or a terrace. But it was more their style. A memory of Mexico. Maybe it would give their backyard the zip it was missing.

Mexican mint. That tastes like a mojito. In their garden.

He planted it in the spring.

It didn't do well at first. It just sat there all that April and May. Even June. Donald said it would shoot up like sugar cane. Donald said it would send out long green shoots. Like a miniature willow.

All spring Dave's mint sat in the backyard garden like a stalk of damp, dwarf corn.

Most people would have lost interest. Most people would have given up, but most people don't have Mary Turlington living next door.

Mary standing on her terrace in her white capris, wine glass in hand. Mary on her hands and knees, with a carpenter's level and her husband, Bert, at the end of a long piece of string. Mary nodding her head in that self-satisfied way of hers. "They're as flat this year as they were last," said Mary, loud enough for everyone to hear.

"No winter heave," she told Dave, and everyone else she ran into. "None at all. Italian workmanship. That terrace could withstand an earthquake."

"I don't know," said Morley one night, looking out their bedroom window, "maybe we should, you know, get some people in, like Mary did."

So, somewhat wistfully, somewhat forlornly, somewhat pathetically, Dave kept at his little project.

He fertilized it. He fed it Miracle-Gro. He tried eggshells and a bucket of compost. Nothing helped.

Then in late June they had five, maybe six days of straight sun. And he didn't check on it, not once, forgot about it, truth be told, and *when* he remembered, maybe two weeks had gone by.

"Come. Come," he said to Morley when she got home that night.

He pulled her into the garden, and they stood there, staring at the mint.

"It grew two or three feet. In a week," he said.

That was the Monday.

Tuesday it grew a foot more. Twelve inches. *Overnight.*

"I can't believe it," said Dave. "It's hard to believe."

By the end of the next week, there was a second stalk standing beside the first. Maybe six inches, a foot away.

He was waiting for Morley in the driveway after work.

"I think I am a father," he said.

"I am very happy for you," said Morley.

And she was. Delighted, though more by his enthusiasm than anything.

By the end of the month, there were a dozen or so babies. Dave's backyard was a fecund hothouse.

It was better than he had ever imagined.

Of course he took the credit for it.

"It was partly the fertilizer," he told Morley, earnestly, one night.

"And partly the earth. Also the goldfish."

"The goldfish?" said Morley.

"The Chudarys' goldfish. I just, you know, I had a feeling."

Morley was frowning at him.

"I buried the Chudarys' goldfish," said Dave. "The one that ..."

Morley held up her hand.

She said, "No details."

Then she got up from the dining-room table. But before she left the room, she turned. "Have you buried anything else? Because if you have, now would be a good time to ... "

Then she interrupted herself.

"Never mind," she said. "I don't want to know."

Dave said, "You understand the goldfish was dead, right?"

Maybe if he had had the remotest idea of what he was doing, maybe if he had a clue about plant behaviour and pruning, or maybe if he had asked someone who did, perhaps what happened this summer could have been avoided. Maybe if Morley had been available, maybe if she hadn't accepted a residency at a summer theatre in cottage country, maybe *she* would have kept him on the rails. But he didn't have a clue about what he was doing. And he didn't ask anyone. And she went away.

It was mid-July when Morley came back from her first few weeks up north and saw what was going on.

"Weren't you going to cut that back?" she asked. "What's going on back there?"

There was no denying that *something* was going on. Instead of thinning out the yard, Dave's pruning had had the opposite effect. It had provoked his plant to a new level of vigour.

"How much mint do you think we need?" said Morley.

Dave had been wondering the same thing.

He went out to the garden and tugged at the smallest plant. He expected it to pop out of the earth like a carrot. To his chagrin, he pulled out a runner, a sort of cable that connected the plant he was tugging on to the one beside it. And then to the one beside that.

He stood there, plant in hand, as the truth dawned on him. All this new growth, all his babies, were not new *plants*. The tendrils, which had grown off the original stalk of mint, had fallen back to the earth, burrowed into the soil, and reappeared as new stalks several feet away. His Mexican mint wasn't having *babies*—it was roaming around his yard like an octopus.

The mint, which had seemed cute and kind of fun, was beginning to scare him.

By the end of the month, it had broken free of the garden perimeter and was heading towards the garage.

It had morphed from an octopus into something closer to a pod of dolphins—dipping and diving across the yard.

At the beginning of August, Dave and Morley and the kids headed up north. Two weeks by the lake.

On the first night away, a year too late, Dave sat down at the computer and typed in three words: *Mexican Climbing Mint.*

He got two words back.

Invasive species.

He looked around the cottage furtively. He didn't want anyone else to see this.

"What's the matter?" asked Morley.

"Nothing," said Dave. "Why?"

"You just said 'uh-oh,'" said Morley.

"There's nothing wrong," said Dave. "Absolutely nothing."

"This is about the mint, isn't it?" said Morley.

It took him hours to get to sleep that night. When he did, he fell into a sweat-drenched dream. He was working in rock and roll again. Managing a group called Purple Loosestrife.

In the dream, the sound man was a mollusc named Leroy. One night, after a show, Leroy sat Dave down and explained that when he was hired, he told everyone he was an oyster, but he was really a zebra mussel.

He said he was tired of living a lie.

It was the worst vacation of Dave's life.

They got back home on a Saturday. When they did, Dave bolted out of the car and through the front door, ran past the living room, and the dining room, and into the kitchen.

Surely it wouldn't be as bad as he had been imagining. He set his bag on the kitchen table and peered out the kitchen window.

It wasn't as bad as he had been imagining.

It was worse.

It was *The Day of the Triffids.*

From inside the house, the mint appeared to be climbing the walls of the garage. Like an ivy. But it wasn't climbing the garage. It was attacking the garage. It had got between the garage door and the ground. It was *in* the garage. There were tendrils entwined around the wheels of all the bikes.

Closer to the house, it had wrapped its way around the back door banister. But not just around the wood—it had worked its way *into* the wood. It had started splitting the banister apart.

It was looped around and around the pear tree.

And most astonishingly, it had gotten in the corner of the laundry-room window and started into the house. How was that even possible? The window was closed. But, there, like a line of ants, was a little tendril, nonetheless.

Then he looked down at his feet and gasped.

When Morley came into the kitchen, he was down on his hands and knees tugging at a green tendril that was growing out of the hot air vent.

That night, Dave went into the backyard with the gardening shears.

By the light of the moon, he cut the mother plant off just above the ground.

It didn't seem to make a whit of difference. The mint was a hydra. It had no beginning. It had no end.

There was only one thing to do. He rolled up his sleeves and got to work. He kept at it for the rest of the month, digging up the mint and hacking at it wherever it appeared.

That's how the stories began. Mary heard him one night when she opened her bedroom window.

"What on earth is he doing back there?" she said to Bert.

And Bert, in bed and already half asleep, Bert, the criminal lawyer, said the first thing that came to his mind. "There's only one kind of gardening that you have to do in the dark," said Bert.

Everyone knew *something* was going on. You would see Dave in the middle of the afternoon, when he should have been at work, standing in the driveway all sweaty, his arms scratched.

"What's up?" said Jim Scoffield when he ran into Dave on the sidewalk.

"Oh, nothing," said Dave. "Nothing's wrong."

"I didn't ask if anything was *wrong*," said Jim to everyone he met.

"Mary Turlington has a theory," said Ted Anderson. "Remember when they went to Mexico?"

Dave was doing his best. His *very* best. And for a time, it seemed like his best was going to be good enough.

Then one evening he was sitting on the back stoop surveying his yard when he was seized by a cold fear.

He stood up. He walked tentatively to the fence and peered into Eugene and Maria's yard. It took a while, but he spotted it. He knew he was going to. In the middle of Eugene and Maria's tomato patch. A single rogue stalk. Maybe two feet tall.

With his heart sinking, Dave got a chair from the kitchen and stood on the chair so he could see into the Turlingtons'.

There, in the middle of the Turlingtons' yard, thrusting through the earthquake-proof Italian terrace, peeking into the sun like a groundhog on a summer prairie—the smallest of stalks. But it was announcing that there were more to come.

In that chilling instant, Dave imagined the entire neighbourhood overrun, like that small English village in his science-fiction nightmare. His mojito mint—toppling fences, overrunning homes.

The return of the jungle.

The end of his life.

He had no time to lose.

That was the night Gerta Lowbeer, well known for her insomnia, spotted Dave slipping out of the Turlingtons' backyard after midnight.

Gerta, who reads too many tabloids for her own good, had long suspected that all men, save for her darling Carl, were weak and easily tempted. She was shocked to have her suspicions confirmed.

But it was right there in front of her. Dave running home. Morley, standing at the back door, with her hands on her hips.

Gerta could hear every word in the church-still of the night.

"I'm sorry," said Dave when he reached his wife. "I thought it was over. I swear, I will put an end to it."

Gerta wasn't the only one. The next night, Maria spotted Dave on his hands and knees in her tomato patch and leapt to her own conclusion. He was stealing tomatoes right off their vines. How long had this been going on?

Maria thought back to the previous fall—to the afternoons she had spent canning. No wonder they had run out of canned tomatoes in January.

Dave confided in Kenny Wong over lunch. He had to talk to someone.

It was Kenny who suggested herbicide.

"You have to bring out the big dog," said Kenny. "I got stuff in the States that you can't buy here."

That night, as the moon rose over the neighbourhood, Dave slipped out the back door, heading for the garage and the industrial-sized bottle of herbicide he'd hidden there. He was wearing his hiking boots, his son's ski goggles and a pair of yellow rubber gloves he had found under the sink.

He looked like a four-year-old boy on the trail of trouble.

The garage was dark.

He went back inside and got a flashlight from the kitchen.

Back in the garage, holding the flashlight in his mouth, he fumbled with the herbicide.

It wouldn't have been the easiest job under the best of circumstances. And these weren't the best of circumstances. The gloves made him clumsy. The goggles obscured his vision.

Yet, he managed to get most of the herbicide into the spray bottle he had found in the basement.

He didn't notice the little puddle that missed the bottle and spilled onto the garage floor.

Or that he stepped into it each time he came back for a refill.

He worked through the night, moving back and forth between his neighbours' backyards and his garage. When he was done, he was tired, but satisfied. He had managed to spray everything that had escaped his yard. He had preserved his neighbours' vegetables and shrubs and flowers before any real harm was done. No one would ever know he and his Mexican Climbing Mint had briefly invaded their gardens.

As the first hint of dawn streaked the sky, he headed into his house. It was a good feeling.

But it was a feeling that only lasted a few hours—until he woke and looked out his bedroom window.

Every lawn, as far as he could see, was scarred by brown crunchy footprints.

They led all around the neighbourhood and directly back to his garage.

One street over, he could see Carl Lowbeer, still in his housecoat, methodically following the footprints.

He was almost at Dave's back gate.

Next door Maria was standing by her back door casting her eyes over the backyard.

He had no choice. He dressed and went outside to face them.

He waved them up the driveway and into the back garden.

There was a moment of some confusion. Everyone talking at cross purposes.

"My tomatoes!" said Maria, "I knew it."

"What will people think," Mary whispered. "I'm embarrassed."

"You should be!" said Gerta, shooting Mary a look.

"Wait," said Dave. "This is all my fault."

"Of course it is!" said Mary, Maria and Gerta in unison.

"Actually," said Dave, looking right at Mary. "It began in *your* backyard."

Maria looked confused. Gerta looked disgusted. Mary looked terrified.

"I was jealous of your terraace," said Dave. "And then we went to Mexico and tried this weed."

Mary squeezed Bert's hand.

"Can we stay here?" she whispered. "Will we be accessories?"

Dave presented himself in the worst possible light. Yet, oddly, by the end, he was the only one who was relatively unscathed.

He expected them to … well, quite frankly, he expected them to be furious.

He was totally unprepared when they were … forgiving.

Forgiveness was the last thing he thought he would get from sanctimonious Mary, but there it was. In fact, she seemed almost … was it possible? Relieved?

Gerta had never seemed so … fond of him.

"You are an honest man," she said.

And Maria? After Gerta said the thing about honesty, Maria said, "Such honesty should be rewarded. I want you to help yourself to as many tomatoes as you want from my garden."

When they were all leaving, she looked at Mary and shrugged.

"He has always been a good neighbour." Then she waved her hand in the air.

"A little strange. But … you know."

And so, in the dog days of August, disaster was averted.

Not for the first time, Dave and Mary tottered back from the abyss of neighbourhood warfare.

"That was a close call," said Dave that night.

They were sitting at the picnic table under the pear tree.

He had made dinner. Burgers on the grill. There had been a shift in weather. A stirring in the trees. There was a welcome coolness to the night.

"I love it out here," said Morley.

Next door old Eugene switched off the light in his garden shed and made his slow way towards his house. The glowing tip of his little cigar leading him on.

Dave raised his hand and waved. Eugene lifted his cane and waved back.

"I wouldn't change this. Not a bit," said Morley.

Across the yard the light in the Lowbeers' kitchen switched off.

Somewhere there was a car horn, and a faraway siren. Summer in the city.

THE BLACK BEAST OF MARGAREE

It's the Black Beast of Margaree! He is going to rip our throats open.
—COLIN MCGREGOR

To get to the Vinyl Cafe, Dave's record store, Dave has to walk by his friend Dorothy's bookstore. He does this every day. Or every day he walks to work, which is pretty *much* every day.

It's Dave's habit to drop in on Dorothy most days. Sometimes he takes her a coffee from Kenny Wong's place—Wong's Scottish Meat Pies. Mostly, he comes empty-handed and mostly he doesn't stay more than a few minutes. But you can build a deep relationship on little moments when those moments add up over years.

So he was in there one morning having one of those endearing conversations that good friends have, talking about nothing he and Dorothy hadn't talked about before, singing the old familiar song of friendship, when he abruptly changed the subject.

"How long has *that* been there?" he said.

He was pointing, over Dorothy's shoulder, at a shelf behind the cash register.

Dorothy didn't turn to look. She didn't have to. Dorothy *knew* what he was talking about. He was talking about the

Jonathan Cape edition of the Ian Fleming novel *Goldfinger*. Number seven in the James Bond series.

Dorothy said, "I didn't know you were a fan of Mr. Bond."

"We go way back," said Dave.

Then he said, "I *want* that book."

"It's a first edition," said Dorothy.

"It's an old friend," said Dave.

"An expensive one," said Dorothy.

"I'll take it," said Dave.

Dave first met James Bond in the town where he was born and raised, Big Narrows, Cape Breton, Nova Scotia.

He didn't meet him in a bookstore, or a movie theatre for that matter, where most people made his acquaintance. There was neither a bookstore nor a movie theatre in the Narrows when Dave grew up. He met Mr. Bond at the most splendid building in the Narrows—the town library.

The library was built and paid for by the coal magnate John W. Tress, in memory of his sister. The Agnes Tress Library is, to this day, the only brick building in the Narrows, sitting, as leisurely as a bank, near the end of Main Street.

It is only a single room, but it is a splendid space. Inside, it has a vaulted ceiling and a balcony with a wrought-iron railing running all around. Outside, it has wooden columns and a stone stairway leading up to the front door. It is out of scale with anything else in the Narrows.

It is the town's pride and joy. And everybody, all a flutter and flurry, showed up the day it opened. The Elks' band played. And there were speeches from the mayor and the local member of parliament. Mr. Tress introduced the new librarian.

She came from North Dormer, Massachusetts. A sultry woman with wavy red hair. She arrived the week before and moved into the librarian's house, which Mr. Tress had built right beside his place. Her name was Charity Royall, and she didn't seem to have any interest in books whatsoever. For the year and a half she lived in the Narrows, she rarely got the library open. And certainly not during regular hours.

Whenever she did show up, people would materialize out of nowhere, as if they had been waiting for her. In those first few years, the citizens of Big Narrows treated the library like an elegant restaurant—no one would dream of going without dressing up. The men in ties and jackets. The women in dresses, or at least a skirt.

There were two marriages, a funeral and a couple of baptisms held under the vaulted library ceiling that first year alone.

A few people even signed out books, though not many. Charity Royall discouraged book borrowing.

Not that anyone minded. Taking books out of the library would have disturbed the perfection of the place. No one wanted to mess it up.

When Charity Royall left the Narrows mysteriously one night, she was replaced by Mr. Russell Montgomery, an earnest bibliophile from Edinburgh.

It was Mr. Montgomery who turned the place around. A fastidious man who believed in doing things by the book, Mr. Montgomery ran the Big Narrows Library for fifty-four years with the intensity that J. Edgar Hoover brought to the FBI.

Russell Montgomery was different, no doubt about it. The Narrows had never seen the likes of him. A square peg in a town of round holes. He wore argyle socks and oxblood brogues and carried tins of fruit drops he had shipped from home.

He might have been a disaster, should have been, but he was adored by all, for his love of literature and his deep commitment to sharing it.

The town used to orbit the library in those days. And Russell Montgomery was the sun king, shining from his throne of books. There are things that still happen in Big Narrows that Mr. Montgomery began. Things like Story Circle for example.

This is when the kindergarten class assembles at the library on Monday mornings for stories. They did when Dave was a boy, and they do today.

Still at Christmas, Mr. Montgomery, who is retired and well into his eighties, reads Clement Clarke Moore's *A Visit from Saint Nicholas*. And at Easter, Beatrix Potter's *Peter Rabbit*. And most famously of all, every Halloween, his pièce de résistance—the fearsome saga of the Black Beast of Margaree, the legend of the mythical doglike creature that he says haunts the hills around the Narrows.

According to Mr. Montgomery, the beast was first spotted by an early settler who lost all his livestock in a single summer— each animal displaying violent throat injuries. The story of the Black Beast isn't written down. Mr. Montgomery heard it himself from the grandson of the original farmer. He tells it extemporaneously, his body swaying back and forth as he does—every kindergarten kid swaying back and forth in time like frightened little metronomes.

Under Mr. Montgomery's guidance, Dave whiled away

hours exploring the treasures of John Tress's library. Mr. Montgomery was his guide. His compass. And his map. Ernest Thompson Seton or Ernest Miller Hemingway; Dr. Livingstone or Dr. Seuss. They were all the same to Mr. Montgomery. Wise in the way of children, Mr. Montgomery would as happily bend Fenton Hardy as Thomas Hardy to his literary purpose, which was to arm children with books. Any books.

There is a little park beside the library, with a stand of sweet-smelling balsam. There are two benches facing each other under the trees' graceful shadows. The summer he was thirteen, Dave read *The Caine Mutiny* sitting on the south-facing bench. When he finished the book, he hiked up behind Macaulay's farm and filled a duffle bag with balsam needles. He put them in his pillow, so his bedroom smelled like the park. He had finished the book, but he didn't want to let it go. Even today, the smell of balsam makes Dave long for the sea.

When he returned the book to Mr. Montgomery, Dave said, "I want another one like that one."

Mr. Montgomery came from a family of fishermen. He had spent time on the water. He knew what he was doing. He had a boy on the line. All he had to do now was set the hook. And that is when he handed Dave *Casino Royale*. The first in the James Bond series. He had been saving the book at his desk for just such a moment. It was the *coup de grâce*.

When Dave walked out of the library with the Bond book in his school bag, Mr. Montgomery suspected Dave was doomed. He was right. Dave galloped through the other three Bonds in the library collection and then handed himself over to Mr. Montgomery. He read anything Mr. Montgomery told him to read. Dickens and Richler. Twain and le Carré.

Now, this was back in the days before television came to the Narrows. If you wanted to go to the movies, you had to drive all the way to the Savoy Theatre in far away Glace Bay—something so improbable, so unlikely, that Dave never considered going to the movies a possibility.

Until the summer *Goldfinger* was released, starring Sean Connery.

There was a contest promoting the movie, with five simple questions. The winner would receive a pair of tickets to opening night at the Savoy. Every kid in the Narrows wanted to win. None of them knew the answers to the questions.

Dave knew he could find the answers in the book. He went to Mr. Montgomery. He begged him to get *Goldfinger,* the book, into the library.

It was while he was waiting for it to arrive from Halifax that disaster struck. Dave returned *Huckleberry Finn* to Mr. Montgomery in "grievous condition." That was Mr. Montgomery's description. "Grievous condition."

"It's just honey," said Dave.

The book was lying on the library desk. Mr. Montgomery's hands were hovering over it. He was snapping his sticky fingers open and closed in distress.

Dave was desperate. "If you set it outside for an afternoon," he said, "the ants will clean it."

Mr. Montgomery wrinkled his nose. "I am putting you on warning," he said. "Be careful."

He pulled out his stamp pad and stamped Dave's library card with a black rat. Three rats and your card was suspended.

Dave got his second rat a week later. He dropped *To Kill a*

Mockingbird into the bathtub. When he returned it, it looked more like an accordion than a book.

Neither Dave nor Mr. Montgomery said *anything* when Dave handed in the book. Mr. Montgomery just shook his head sadly and reached for his stamp pad.

Billy Mitchell found the bird the very next afternoon. It was a swallow. He found it in the lane, back of the laundromat, beside the Maple Leaf Restaurant.

It had stunned itself flying into Art Gillespie's office window. Billy carried the bird around in a shoebox for a couple of hours, showing it to everyone. Then, egged on by Warren Sarauer, he took it to the library with a plan to set it loose from the upper balcony. Unfortunately, Dave was up there when they arrived, poring over a well-thumbed copy of *National Geographic*.

Billy handed Dave the box. "Check it out," he said.

When Dave opened the box, the swallow flapped out with a squawk. It flew around and around the domed ceiling, banging up against the glass roof, feathers flying.

When Mr. Montgomery looked up, Dave was standing beside the railing, holding the box. Billy Mitchell and Warren Sarauer had vanished.

Dave said, "It wasn't *my* idea."

Mr. Montgomery suspended his card for a month.

Dave hated Mr. Montgomery.

His card was still under suspension when *Goldfinger* arrived.

Dave didn't have to go into the library to know the book was there. Mr. Montgomery put the book jacket in the display case by the front door, where Dave would be sure to see it. It looked amazing. There was a skull in a pine box, with coins in its empty eye sockets and a rose between its teeth. It was the same jacket that Dorothy had on her shelf behind the cash.

Dave went to the library after school.

Mr. Montgomery was sitting under an umbrella. The swallow was perched at the top of the domed roof directly above him.

Dave ducked under the umbrella and asked Mr. Montgomery to make an exception. Just that book. Just this once.

Mr. Montgomery told him he couldn't sign it out until his suspension was over.

Dave begged, "Can I sit in the library? Can I read it in the library?"

Mr. Montgomery looked puzzled. "But how would you get in the library?" he asked. "You have no library privileges."

Getting in was easy.

He got in the next night—through the coal chute.

Saturday night. Eight-thirty. Everything shut up tight. Down the alley behind the library. In and out in under five minutes.

His plan was simple. He would plow through the book and return it Sunday night. No one would get hurt. No one would even know it was missing. It was risky, but not too risky. Not when you considered what was at stake.

What he wasn't counting on was a novel featuring a villain who is the richest man in England, the world's top gold smuggler, and the treasurer for the Soviet assassination agency SMERSH. We are talking nuclear warheads at Fort Knox. Torture. And a gold-plated Rolls Royce. *Goldfinger* is the novel in which the martial arts expert, Odd Job, is sucked out the window of the jet plane. It is the book that features an

all-female criminal organization called The Cement Mixer—
led by (oh my sweet adolescent heart be still) Miss Pussy
Galore!

He had to read it twice.

He modified his plan. He would return the book Monday
morning at recess.

Monday was Story Circle, of course, so the kindergarten
kids would be there. Dave decided he would take his dog
Scout with him and use Scout as a distraction. Scout loved
kids; kids loved Scout. Whenever Scout saw kids, he would
bound towards them, his tongue out, ready to lick.

Getting a dog down a coal chute is harder than you would
think.

On Monday, at recess, Dave was in the alley behind the
library, hoisting Scout up, trying to shove the dog's bottom
through the chute door. Scout was hunching and scrabbling
and doing his best not to go down.

"Scout," said Dave.

He leaned into him. They passed some critical point, some
point of no return, and off they went—a tumble of dog and boy
that landed with a thud on the coal room floor. There was dust
everywhere, and the two of them, peering at each other in the
gloom of the basement.

If dogs could grin, surely that is what Scout did. He grinned,
and he barked, and he began bounding around the coal room,
tail wagging, trammelling all the coal dust beneath his feet. A
picture of excitement and joy disappearing into the clouds of
black dust.

"Scout," said Dave, trying to calm him.

But there was no calming Scout. He was barking with abandon. His tail was wagging. When he saw the stairs, he headed right for them.

Upstairs, the children in Story Circle were, one by one, tuning in to the commotion, the banging and rumbling that was coming from beneath them. And now, they were turning towards the source, towards the basement door. Not all of them, but at least half. And when half of them were staring at the door, the door burst open and Scout exploded into the library, barking—a black cloud of dust-choked energy. And in the midst of the dusty black whirlwind, two blazing green eyes, a set of long white teeth and a guttural howl that sounded like a werewolf.

It was Colin McGregor who recognized what it was. It was Colin who stood and pointed. It was Colin who screamed, "It's the Black Beast of Margaree!"

Colin flung himself at the nearest shelf of books and started scrambling up. "He is going to rip our throats open," screamed Colin.

Others followed, kicking books off the shelves as they climbed. Only Colin made it to the top.

As soon as he got there, the shelf began to rock slowly back and forth. Colin stood at the top, like the soldier on the apex of a war memorial, and rode the falling bookcase all the way down.

Mr. Montgomery and his umbrella were buried by the avalanche of flying books.

When he surfaced, there was a moment of complete and utter silence. And then, to add to the indignation, the swallow sensed its chance, swooped around the room once and made a deposit on Mr. Montgomery's forehead.

In the commotion, no one spotted Dave standing at the top of the stairs. When *he* saw the shelf coming down, he turned and ran down the stairs and through the coal room door. He hurled himself at the chute. He was still clutching *Goldfinger*.

He dropped it halfway up and watched it tumble back into the coal bin. He wasn't going back for it, that's for sure.

Not for the book. And not for Scout. Scout was on his own.

Of course, Dave never entered the contest. Having read the book, he knew all the answers. But he couldn't let on. If he had entered the contest, he would have won it. And Mr. Montgomery would have figured out that was him in the library that morning.

Billy Mitchell won the trip to Glace Bay. Billy who found the swallow. Where is the justice in that?

"**A**nd that is about all of it," said Dave.

"A good story," said Dorothy.

"A long time ago," said Dave.

He was sitting on the stool that Dorothy has by her cash register. He opened the copy of *Goldfinger* that she had handed him. He began flipping through it.

"I always loved the part where Odd Job went out the window.

"Did you know he wrote *Chitty Chitty Bang Bang*?" asked Dave.

"Did you know he was a friend of Noel Coward?" asked Dorothy.

"A great character," said Dave. "Real colour. I read once that he was the guy who concocted the plot that lured Rudolf Hess into flying to Scotland. I don't know if that is true."

He glanced down at the book. "Thirteen novels. He only lived long enough to see two of the films."

Then he looked at his watch. He said, "I have to go."

The letter came a month later. A white form letter, in a white envelope, postmarked Big Narrows.

> *Thank you for your kind donation of* Goldfinger *by Ian Fleming. The book has been catalogued and added to our stacks. It is now in circulation and available for our members to borrow. It is through donations such as yours that our library remains a vital part of the community.*

There was a p.s. at the bottom written with a fountain pen in a spidery hand.

> *David, to answer your question, the library is open Monday, Wednesday and Friday afternoons. There is no longer a permanent librarian. It is run by a committee and staffed by volunteers. I still do the circle on special occasions. Aside from the hours, nothing much has changed since you were a boy. We haven't bought any new books for well over a decade, although people do donate books from time to time. Your cheque is most appreciated and will be added to a fund to make some general repairs, most critically to the roof.*

> *I checked, and we do have all thirteen books in the Bond series. Plus the short stories. Our copy of* Goldfinger, *however, is damaged. It looks as if*

*it has been set afire. Although you already knew
that, didn't you? We will replace our copy with the
one you sent. We will sell the damaged one in our
autumn sale, and I would be delighted to buy it for
you as you requested. I will keep it at the house for
when you are next in town.*

*Thank you again. I saw your mother and told her
about your kind donation. She said you always
liked the library, and you spoke fondly of me.
Thank you for that.*

It was signed, *Russell Montgomery.*

Dave read the letter twice. Then he folded it carefully and
put it in the drawer below the cash.

That night, on his way home, he stopped at the video store
and rented a movie.

"Have you seen it?" he asked Morley when he got home.

"James Bond?" she said.

"An early one," said Dave. "*Goldfinger.* One of the ones with
Sean Connery ..."

"I thought you had seen them all?" she said.

"Not this one," said Dave.

CURSE OF
THE CRAYFISH

The fragrance of dead crayfish. Mmm-mm."
—KENNY WONG

When Gerta finally figured it out—well, it seemed so obvious, she couldn't *believe* it took her so long.

She figured it out in the spring. Carl, her husband Carl, had become distant and moody again.

"You could *almost* say depressed."

"I am *not* depressed," said Carl.

"Exactly like *last* spring," said Gerta.

And that's when she put it together.

"You miss the fishing game," said Gerta.

For twenty-two years Carl had organized the company's fishing contest.

"Team," said Carl. "I organized the team. I was the team captain. And it wasn't a game. It was a tournament."

For twenty-two years Carl had organized the company team for the Big Bear Fishing Derby. And then Carl had retired.

"You make it sound like it was my idea," said Carl. "I would have kept working."

And that is the rub. Carl never wanted to retire. And when he did, or more to the point, when he turned sixty-five and was forced to, it never occurred to him that he would be dropped from the fishing derby roster. It was as much *his* thing as the company's, for heaven's sake. It wasn't as if the derby was … *business.*

What was most galling was that he still received invitations to the company barbecue, the company golf tournament and even the fall food drive.

Carl suspected Norm Harrison was behind his exclusion. Norm had settled into Carl's office before Carl had moved his last box out. Norm had been manoeuvring for a spot on the fishing team for years.

"The derby is a big deal," said Carl. "If you knew *anything* about fishing, you'd know it is a deal."

"Right," and Gerta.

And during his last five years as captain?

"We came second," said Carl. "Twice. And third once. We were … overdue."

"But you never won," said Gerta.

"We would have," said Carl.

And that is how Carl, Bert Turlington, Kenny Wong and Dave came to find themselves shoe-horned into Room 24 of the Red Squirrel Motel and Cabins. It was one of those places where the wafer of soap, the *one* wafer, comes wrapped in pale green paper, with a picture of a squirrel gnawing on a pine cone.

At least Bert figured it was the soap.

"*This* is the soap?" asked Bert. "Not a pat of butter?"

It was the last room in the only place with a room left. Everything else was booked solid.

"We were lucky to get it," said Carl.

Two double beds.

Four grown men.

Dave and Kenny were sharing the bed next to the door. Bert and Carl had the other one.

At five the next morning, Carl opened his eyes.

Dave was already up.

"It's raining," said Dave.

This was more or less the beginning of it.

Five in the morning, in the rain, Room 24 of the Red Squirrel Motel, 45 kilometres from Lake Boirreau.

They had two days.

Each team was allowed to submit four fish. The rest had to be thrown back. There were two prizes: one for the biggest single fish, the other for the team with the biggest total—by weight.

Registration was at the marina. The marina was about half an hour away.

"Those are the guys," said Carl. "That's Norm Harrison. I knew it."

Carl's old office team.

There were four of them—loading stuff into a low-profile fishing boat with twin 75-horsepower Mercs. One of those fancy bow-riders with chairs. The kind you see on the television fishing shows.

They were wearing matching khaki vests. And green matching ball caps. All of them had so much gear hanging from their belts, they looked more like they were heading out to repair phone lines than catch fish.

Carl made a sorry sight, standing there in the rain, holding his Styrofoam cup of worms.

Of course it was Norm Harrison who spotted him.

"Whoa, Carl Lowbeer," said Norm. "I didn't know you were still around. Sure didn't expect to see *you* here. Hey boys, it's Carl Lowbeer."

"I hate those guys," muttered Carl a few minutes later. "I'll show them who's still around."

Carl was standing at the far end of the dock, beside a sixteen-foot aluminum boat with an old, blue ten-horsepower Evinrude.

"There was nothing else left," said Carl. "We were lucky to get it."

The boat was filled with six inches of skuzzy brown water. Dave climbed in, picked up a yogourt container floating in the bottom, sat on the far gunwale and began to bail. The water was cold. His hands were freezing.

Half an hour later, a short heavy guy with a Fu Manchu moustache and a yellow rain suit waved an air horn over his head, gave it a blast, and the boats coughed to life and roared into the fog.

Only one was left behind—Dave and Bert and Kenny sitting there glumly, watching as Carl pulled the starting cord again and again. The heavy guy with the Fu Manchu moustache walked over.

"Too much choke," he said. "You've flooded her."

When they finally swamped off and out into Big Bay, their gunwales were no more than two inches above the surface of the lake. They sputtered out of the marina, Dave still bailing, the guy in the yellow jacket standing there shaking his head.

They were looking for smallmouth bass, a relatively small fish (two pounds is a good size, anything over four—a wall hanger), yet said by bass aficionados to be, pound for pound, the greatest fighting fish in the world. They were heading for a bay that Carl liked—through a narrows, and around a point, and then left by a flat rock at the end of the lake.

"Lots of low trees," shouted Carl over the motor. "And deadfalls. Bass like shade."

It was only seven-thirty when they got there. And raining harder.

They took turns. Three fishing. One bailing.

It wasn't the greatest of beginnings. Bert, who had never fished before, not once, not ever, kept getting hung on snags. Carl had to cut his line three times; each cut meant sacrificing a spinner Carl would have rather kept. And then, around ten, Bert bird-nested his line, and the only way to fix it was to cut it off the reel and throw the whole mess out.

That wasn't the worst of it. The worst of it was that the two fishermen in the boat, the two guys who knew what they were doing—Kenny and Carl—disagreed on just about everything there is to disagree with when it comes to fishing.

Carl moved slowly. Carl threw his line out methodically and brought it back on a long, slow retrieve. Carl believed the way to catch fish was to keep a line in the water.

Kenny, on the other hand, was the busiest fisherman you have ever seen. Kenny was trying something different every two minutes. Going fast, going slow. Trying this lure. Trying that one. Kenny was in constant motion.

But worst of all (or worst of all as far as Carl was concerned) was that Kenny kept suggesting they try somewhere else, change bays.

Kenny was driving Carl nuts.

It stopped raining at ten-thirty.

At eleven the sun was out and the lake misty, and they peeled off their jackets.

The bugs came out with the sun.

They were bad, but not unbearable. They were sort of hot and swatty, bothersome and irritating, annoying rather than vexing, until, that is, Kenny opened a can of pop, and it exploded.

It exploded all over Carl, turning Carl into a sticky, sugary fly magnet.

Five minutes later, five minutes after he had doused Carl, Kenny caught the first fish. It was around noon.

Carl said, "Toss it back."

Kenny looked at it and shrugged. It was about one and a half pounds. Carl was the boss. Kenny threw it back. They didn't even take a picture.

In the middle of the afternoon, it started to rain again.

By four it was coming down pretty steadily.

Bert looked at Dave. Dave looked at Kenny. Kenny shrugged and pointed at Carl.

Carl said, "Yeah. Okay."

And they put their rods away, and they started the engine, and they headed back.

Halfway to the marina, Carl's old team zoomed by in their flat-bottomed pro boat. The big boat was almost planing, the bow bouncing up and down ever so slightly. The four passengers were sitting under the bimini, looking dry and satisfied.

As the fibreglass vessel skimmed by the tiny aluminum boat, Norm Harrison reached down and held up a string of fish.

Carl eyeballed it.

"The one at the bottom's got to be close to four pounds," said Carl glumly.

As wet and cold as day one had been, day two felt blessed.

In fact their second morning was so different from the morning before that Carl found it hard to believe he was in the same world, at the same place, doing the same thing.

It was a half hour before dawn when they pulled into the marina. Even as he walked onto the dock, Carl sensed a certain grace had settled upon them.

The motor started with the first pull.

"A beautiful thing," said Carl.

It was still dark as they putted away.

Out in Big Bay, Carl pointed to a bull moose swimming across the lake, his huge head and antlers a shadow against the dark shore.

Twenty minutes later, they pulled into their bay and surprised a raft of ducks. Carl heard them before he saw them—their surprised coughs, and then the beat of their wings as they lifted up and skidded down a safe distance away.

The songbirds were only just starting to wake.

Carl opened the bag at his feet and handed everyone a cup of coffee. He passed around a bag of muffins. They floated there happily as the sky turned an impossible palette of pinks and powder blues.

By eleven they had two fish—neither of them huge, but both big enough to keep, both big enough to ratchet up the level of intensity. Maybe they *could* win this.

Kenny was spraying his lure with a little aerosol bottle.

"That stuff smells horrible," said Dave.

"Not to a fish," said Kenny. "The fragrance of dead crayfish. Mmm-mm."

At eleven-thirty Kenny was proved right. He hooked his second fish. This one hit hard. Kenny jerked his rod, and the fish jumped high, twisting in the air on the way down.

"Good lord," said Carl.

"Tip down. Tip down," said Carl.

"It's got to be *four pounds*," said Carl, as Kenny played his line out.

It weighed five. Five pounds, four ounces.

"I don't remember anything over four. Ever," said Carl. "It could be a record."

The fish went into the bucket in the centre of the boat. They still had six more hours. They didn't want it drying out. They didn't want to risk losing even a precious ounce of moisture.

At noon they were floating there, their feet up again, eating sandwiches, feeling ... not smug, exactly, but clearly pleased with themselves.

"One more good-sized fish, and we have a shot at this," said Carl. Carl's knee was bouncing up and down. Carl was excited.

"Take that, Norm Harrison," muttered Carl under his breath.

And that is when Dave pointed at a little weedy shallow and said, "If I was a fish, I would hide in there."

Where it was cool. Where there would be stuff to eat. Where nothing would eat you.

It wasn't such a bad idea.

Carl had a pair of hip waders in his pack. Carl put the waders on.

They poled over and put him ashore on a rock. He waded into the weeds.

He worked at it for about twenty minutes, the water up to his knees. He waved at them in the boat. Nothing yet. He waded out further.

The pressure of the lake pressed the waders against his body. It felt as if he were being squeezed. Like he was wearing pressure socks. It felt like the lake was hugging him. Like he was *of* the lake rather than in it.

He moved deeper—almost up to his waist. Standing there in the weeds. Long slow casts. Long slow retrieves.

The rhythm of it was completely absorbing. Draw the rod back, throw the line out, reel the line in. Draw the rod back. Throw the line out. It was like a dance. One, two, three. One, two, three.

Time passed. How much? Who knew?

A dragonfly landed on a lily pad in front of him.

There was a splash about fifty yards to his right. Something had broken the water to his right. Whatever it was, Carl sensed it was big.

It jumped again. Carl spooled in quickly, about to wade over, when he remembered the spray Kenny had slipped in his pocket as he was climbing out of the boat.

"Try this," Kenny had said.

He pulled the plastic bottle out of his pocket and shrugged. He gave his lure a few quick sprays. He glanced at his watch. Four o'clock. They had two hours left. Most of the afternoon had passed. It was now or never. On an impulse, Carl gave *himself* a blast from the aerosol.

He thought it might mask his odour. He sprayed his back, his shoulders and his arms.

Carl was convinced they were one fish away from the championship. That *one fish* might be a cast away. Landing it would be like hitting a home run in the ninth inning of the last game in the World Series.

He was wading over to where the fish had jumped, trying not to splash, trying to glide.

When he thought he was close enough, he stopped, lifted his rod, drew it back over his right shoulder and cast out the line.

The lure hit the water. He let the lure settle and he began to reel it in.

Later he would swear he could feel the bass breathing on his line.

But it didn't bite.

It didn't do anything.

A second cast.

Then a third.

On the fourth he felt it again. But this time there was more than just breath.

There was ... something.

A *tap*.

Another *tap*.

A *tap tap*.

Carl stopped breathing.

There *was* something there.

This was it. This was his moment. Carl inhaled deeply. Waiting. Waiting.

Another *tap*.

And ...

"Okay, Norm Harrison," said Carl under his breath, and he broke his wrists, and jerked his arms back to set the hook.

His rod shook. There was a flash of silver three feet above the water—the fish twisting against the sky like an acrobat.

He felt the weight right away. It was at least as big as Kenny's. It was four pounds if it was two.

And *that* is when he saw the bear.

It was sitting on the shore, maybe thirty yards away. Sitting like a bear in a children's story, its back slumped over, its paws between its legs. The bear was watching the fish as intently as Carl was.

Tip down. Reel in.

The fish jumped.

The bear stood up.

The bear charged through the shallow water, towards the fish.

Carl watched in horror as the bear flicked his fish into the air and caught it in its mouth. The fish that was still attached to the end of Carl's line.

As the bear turned and scrambled towards shore, Carl's fishing line screamed and began to unravel.

Possession, as they say, is nine-tenths of the law. Possession can do strange things to a man.

That was *Carl's* fish.

Carl gave his line a mighty jerk.

"That's *mine*," said Carl.

The notion that he no longer actually *had* a fish on his line hadn't sunk in. The notion that he had a bear on his line didn't sink in until later.

Carl set his legs and jerked again.

The bear, who had been loping for the shore, stopped dead, and glanced over its shoulder.

A look of amazement clouded its face. It stood up on its back legs, its body swaying slightly, its snout in the air, testing the wind.

Carl and the bear realized *what* it was smelling at exactly the same instant.

Her favourite thing in the world.

Dead crayfish.

"Uh-oh." said Carl.

It is a dangerous and controversial thing to assign feelings to animals. But anyone who has ever owned a dog, or been around a dog when a dog treat is dangled in front of her, knows that dogs are capable of desire and longing.

Carl would tell you bears are too. Because Carl saw desire and longing cross the bear's face.

Or was it lust?

The bear was looking at the largest crayfish it had ever seen.

It was Kenny who spotted them.

Or more to the point, the bear. On all fours. Leaping through the water towards Carl.

It was Kenny who barked at Bert to start the motor.

And while Bert fumbled with the engine, it was Kenny who realized they weren't going to make it in time.

It was Kenny who bought them the time they needed by scooping his five-pound champion bass out of the bucket and throwing the fish as hard as he could. It hit the bear on the chest—just as the motor roared to life.

The bear snagged the fish as it fell towards the water, as they drove by her at full speed. No more than ten yards away.

"Closer," said Dave later that night. "I felt her breath. I could smell her."

Dave and Kenny dragged Carl over the gunwales on the fly, as the bear turned and carried the prize fish to shore.

They watched from the water as she ate it on the beach and then as she stood up and melted into the forest.

Later, that night, later on Sunday night, they were standing in a little group in their motel parking lot.

They had come in two cars. Both cars were packed. They were ready to go.

The sun was down. Carl's defeat by bear had been somewhat mollified by the thrill of escape.

"I swear we were close enough that I smelled her breath," said Dave, for maybe the tenth time.

Their defeat had also been mollified by the calamity that had befallen Norm Harrison and the team representing Carl's former workplace.

"I don't," said Carl, "like to ... you know ..."

"Celebrate someone else's misfortunes," said Dave.

"Yes," said Carl. "But ..."

"But when *they* were the agents of their *own* decline," said Dave.

"It's hard not to ... you know," said Carl.

"Gloat?" said Dave.

Norm Harrison's team had been caught using a worm blower—a little device that inflates worms and makes them float off the bottom and into the strike zone. A flagrant transgression in this feel-good derby. Norm Harrison had been disqualified.

And so Carl and his team went home. Not exactly champions.

"Almost champions," said Carl. And not altogether unpleased with themselves.

They got together to celebrate a month later—at Kenny's café, after closing.

The four of them sat in the booth in the corner. A platter of crispy spring rolls, a whole steamed fish with garlic and ginger, broccoli in a spicy pepper sauce, a bottle of red wine, in front of them.

"To the bear," said Dave, holding up his glass. "I swear I smelled its breath."

They all hoisted their glasses, and when they had drunk, Dave looked at Kenny and nodded ever so slightly.

Kenny got up and disappeared through the swinging doors into the kitchen. When he came back, he was carrying a package wrapped in brown paper.

He shoved the brown paper package into Carl's hands.

"It's from all of us," he said.

Carl looked at the package and then at the three of them sitting there.

"Go ahead," said Bert. "Unwrap it."

They had got their hands on a perfect fish skeleton. They

had had the skeleton mounted on a plaque. Like a taxidermied trophy.

Carl laughed.

"Bones of the bass," he said.

There was a gold plaque screwed onto the trophy.

Carl read it out loud.

> *Many people go fishing all their lives without knowing that it's not fish they are after.*

"Thoreau," said Bert.

"I have never read Thoreau," said Carl.

Then Carl said, "Maybe we should try again. Next year. "

"That's the idea," said Dave. "We have already reserved a room."

"One room?" asked Carl, in despair.

"All for one. One for all," said Dave.

And he reached out with his spoon and scooped the last of the ginger garlic sauce off the plate.

"I swear," he said. "I smelled her breath."

WHATEVER HAPPENED TO JOHNNY FLOWERS?

So I didn't actually drop him. The mayor straightened for the camera, the flashbulbs went off and the baby sort of slithered out of my arms.
—DAVE

Dave was standing by the back door of his record store, leaning against the door frame, gazing over the picnic table at the brave little trees that grow back there, at the garbage cans, and the recycling bins, at the cracked concrete of the narrow alleyway, and mostly, at the water pooling everywhere. It had been raining all morning, and it didn't look like it was going to stop anytime soon.

He called out when he spotted his pal, Kenny, running down the alley holding a newspaper over his head. Kenny Wong, who owns the little café half a block along—Wong's Scottish Meat Pies.

"Kenny," shouted Dave.

Kenny, turning and spotting the open door, changed direction and ducked in.

"Geez," said Kenny, shaking himself off.

"You can say *that* again," said Dave, taking the soaked newspaper and dropping it onto a pile of boxes. "Coffee?"

Kenny said, "Coffee would be nice."

They headed from the back room into the cramped comfort of the store. Dave picked up a mug from a shelf, sniffed it suspiciously and then filled it with coffee from the pot.

"Is it clean?" asked Kenny.

Dave ignored the question and handed the mug to Kenny. "Has it ever occurred to you," he said, "that when *you* come *here,* you get coffee for free? Yet when *I* go to *your* place, I *pay* for it? Does that not strike you as a little weird?"

"Not at all," said Kenny, examining his mug carefully.

"And why is that?" said Dave, holding out a carton of cream.

"Because *I'm* ... a professional," said Kenny, sniffing the cream. "And *you* ... are an amateur."

"I wouldn't be an amateur if you *paid* for your coffee," said Dave.

Kenny shrugged and pointed at the box on Dave's desk. "Is that the box?" he asked.

"Yeah," said Dave.

It was a lacquered wood box, smaller, as they say, than a breadbox. Dark brown, with a reddish flare, and a gold fastener. A piece of craftsmanship.

Dave was fiddling with the fastener.

"I was in a second-hand store in Bridgewater," said Dave. "Looking for records. When I saw it, there was something ... I don't know. It looked ... familiar. Anyway I opened it."

Like he was opening it now. And when it was open, he reached in, like he had reached in that afternoon in the second-hand store in Bridgewater, and he pulled out a silver mug. He handed it to Kenny.

Kenny said, "It's a christening mug."

"There's an inscription," said Dave.

Kenny read it out loud:

In celebration of one hundred years
Big Narrows, Cape Breton
Centenial baby

"It's the *centennial* mug," said Dave.

Kenny said, "*Centennial* is spelled wrong. There should be another *n*."

"Yeah," said Dave, "that was the mayor. Anyway. It was presented to the centennial baby. I was there when they gave it to him."

Then he said, "It's a long story."

Kenny pointed at the window. It was still raining.

Dave said, "It's such a long time ago."

Dave was three the summer Big Narrows, the town where he grew up, turned one hundred years old. So he doesn't remember much, but he had heard all the stories—from his parents, from the older kids in town. There was so much going on. Looking back, it is hard to believe it all. They built the fountain at the base of the war memorial. They paved the road all the way past Macaulay's farm.

And the centennial parade! People came from as far away as Sydney to watch the parade. There was a guy from Quebec who carved a massive ice sculpture of a cod. He worked on it behind the laundromat for two days straight. When it was finished, it was almost as big as the mayor. Or at least it was at the start of the parade. The Boy Scouts pulled it in the back of the Gillespies' old ice wagon. Right in front of the town's fire truck, which had its siren going. And as if *that* wasn't enough excitement, the parade was led by the king of England himself.

"The king?" asked Kenny. "King *Elizabeth*?"

"Well, the kids all thought it was the king," said Dave. "You know, when you are little, you can get details like that muddled."

He was actually an earl. A distant cousin of the queen. He was supposed to bring his wife, the countess, and it was his wife who was supposed to lead the parade, wearing an emerald tiara. But the countess refused to come.

"Canada?" said the countess. "In August? Give your head a shake."

"If not August," said the earl, "when?"

"Exactly," said the countess.

So the earl, who turned out to be a drinking buddy of Stone McConnell's during the war, arrived alone. He agreed to lead the parade himself on account of some debt he owed Stone. Anyway, he arrived a couple of days early and pretty much spent them all drinking whisky sours in the Starlight Room at the Breakwater Hotel.

When the big moment arrived, the earl was pretty moony, and by all accounts, didn't need much persuading to stuff himself into Jolene McLauchlin's wedding dress.

He led the parade, wearing the wedding dress and the tiara, and waving at everyone in that stiff royal way.

"When you're a kid," said Dave, "you can miss the humour in that sort of thing. Anyway, that's not what I wanted to tell you about. The point of all this is not the parade. It's the centennial baby. It was supposed to be Annie."

"Your sister," said Kenny.

Well, that's what everyone in town thought at the time. When you consider the facts, you can hardly blame them. Centennial weekend was the first weekend in August. Dave's mother, Margaret, was due that very week. No one else in town was expecting until September. There had already been a picture of Margaret in *The Antigonish Casket*, and weekly updates in *The Community News*. There was a big basket of prizes waiting to be presented to her, and the mug, of course, which had been ordered from the Birks jewellery store in Montreal. "The school kids went on a field trip just to see it," said Dave.

"They went to Montreal?" asked Kenny. "To see the mug?"

"No, no," said Dave. "It arrived in town in the spring. They had it on display at the library."

It was in the glass case, by the front door—where they usually displayed the new books. You could tell just by looking at it that it was worth a lot. The rumour was maybe $50. Kenny spun the mug around in his hands. It was tarnished, almost bronze coloured near the handle.

"It was a big deal," said Dave. "Everyone just assumed that mug was ours."

So it was a complete shock, to everyone, when Digger and Lulu Flowers showed up at the hospital on the third of August—and Lulu was in labour. Lulu wasn't due until the middle of September. But a burst of water, an hour of wailing, some rushing around and it was all over; Digger and Lulu's five-and-a-half-pound son, Johnny, was the centennial baby.

"Annie was born three days later," said Dave.

The presentation of the centennial mug was scheduled for the fairgrounds on the night of the centennial parade.

"Someone decided it would be nice to have me on stage," said Dave. "As some sort of consolation, I guess. And when the choir was singing 'God Save the Queen,' and they were about to give Lulu the mug, the mayor thought it would be cute if they got a picture of me and the baby. And to make a long story short, I dropped him."

"They let a three-year-old hold a baby?" asked Kenny.

"I was sitting in a chair. They put the baby in my lap. The mayor was hanging on to him too," said Dave. "So I didn't technically drop him. The mayor straightened for the camera, the flashbulbs went off and the baby sort of slithered out of my arms. Or at least that's what I've been told.

"Okay. I dropped him."

"Good lord," said Kenny. "Was he okay?"

"He grew up to be a little punk of a kid ... and I always wondered ..."

"You thought it was your fault," said Kenny.

"Yeah," said Dave. "He was always getting in trouble. Picking on kids, picking fights. Everyone was scared of Johnny Flowers. I was three years older than him, and *I* was scared of him."

"Great name for a little hoodlum," said Kenny.

"He *was* a little hoodlum," said Dave. "He wore a black leather vest. And he used to carry a can of chewing tobacco, tucked into his pants, behind his belt buckle. And I always felt guilty," said Dave. "Like he had turned out rotten because I dropped him. Like I had damaged him in some way."

"What happened to him?" asked Kenny.

"Well that's the point," said Dave. "I don't know. He disappeared. Left town. The whole family left. I never saw him again. Or even heard about him. And *that* belongs to him. Not to me."

Dave was pointing at the mug.

Big feelings, feelings that make themselves perfectly clear, are sometimes hard to understand perfectly clearly. What *was* perfectly clear was that Dave had been taken over by this mug, which his family had once believed was going to be awarded to them, and which, through some strange quirk of the world, had made its way, all these years later, into his possession. Dave had become obsessed with the mug.

He talked about it all the time.

"I think it's pretty clear," said Kenny. "It's a guilt thing. You're being driven by guilt."

Whatever it was, all Dave knew was that he wanted to get the mug back into the possession of the person to whom it rightfully belonged. But trying to find someone who has vanished from your life is not as easy as you might think.

Where do you start? If a starting point was obvious, then you couldn't really say the person had vanished. You could say, maybe, that they had drifted away, or that you had drifted apart. Clouds drift. But Johnny Flowers wasn't a cloud; Johnny Flowers was a rifle shot, a puff of smoke. He was gone. After a while, the answer to where you start becomes clearer. You start with what you know. Dave bought a little notebook and wrote Johnny Flowers's name on the cover. What did he know about Johnny Flowers? Maybe if he wrote it down, he could see it better.

Well, he knew his birthday. Or he knew how to find it. Dave phoned his sister, Annie.

"When's your birthday?" he asked.

"Why?" said Annie, suspiciously.

And so he told her about the mug, and how he wanted to return it to Johnny Flowers.

"That was supposed to be *my* mug," said Annie.

She made him guess her birthday. It took him seven tries.

He went back to his list and under Johnny Flowers's name, he wrote *date of birth: August 3rd*. Then he wrote down the year his sister was born.

Next he phoned MacDonnell's, Big Narrows's general store, video shop and, most importantly, post office.

He asked to speak to Elizabeth.

Elizabeth said of course she remembered the Flowers family. "The centennial baby. It should have been your sister. He was a little menace, that one."

And, no, they hadn't received mail for them for years.

"I think they moved to Alberta," said Elizabeth.

Dave phoned information and asked for the listing of J. Flowers. Any J. Flowers.

The lady told him she would need a town.

"It could be anywhere," said Dave.

She said, "I have twenty-one across Canada."

He called them all.

"Are you the Johnny Flowers from Big Narrows?" he asked.

None of them were. And none of them knew who he was talking about. The Flowers family of Big Narrows, Nova Scotia, was gone, gone, gone.

He kept at his notebook. Whenever he remembered *anything* about Johnny Flowers, he wrote it down. At the end of two weeks, he had written pages of things. Things like this:

Johnny Flowers was a punk.

Johnny Flowers smoked Export A.

Johnny Flowers's father drove the coolest car that has ever been built. A goldenrod-yellow 1955 Ford Thunderbird. The two-seater from the very first year the Thunderbird was made.

A week after he'd remembered the car, he sat down at the computer and typed in *1955 Ford Thunderbird, Nova Scotia.* Before he knew it, he was staring at a list of people who were buying and selling used Thunderbird parts. And there, right in front of his eyes, the third item on the list:

Wanted: 1955 FORD THUNDERBIRD IGNITION SWITCH

Beneath it was the name: *J. Flowers of Sagmouch, New Brunswick.* And a phone number.

It was Johnny, of course. Who else could it be? He still had his father's car. You would never sell a car like that.

It took Dave three weeks to get up the courage to call.

Finally one night when he was out walking Arthur, the dog, instead of going to the park as he usually would, he went back to the store and quietly let himself in. He turned on the small lamp by the phone, but no other lights, and in the dim yellow glow of the lamp, he dialed the New Brunswick number. Johnny Flowers answered on the second ring. When he did, Dave hung up. He hung up and sat staring at the phone.

He would write instead.

Ten minutes later, he picked up the phone again.

"Johnny Flowers?" he said.

"Yes?"

"From Big Narrows?"

"Who is this?"

"That was me who just called."

"We were cut off," said Johnny. "I didn't hang up."

"I know you didn't," said Dave. "I did."

There was a silence, which Dave eventually filled.

"I'm not sure if you will remember me. It's Dave. Margaret's son. Annie's brother."

"You're the guy that dropped me."

"That's me," said Dave.

"I have a scar."

"You're kidding."

They talked for over an hour.

Johnny Flowers said, "I didn't fit into that town. I don't like to remember the place. I feel like I was just a big disappointment to everyone. They all expected the worst of me."

And just like that, Dave was back in the Narrows—back in MacDonnell's General Store—a teenager again. It was a summer night. They had been playing baseball in the park, and he and Billy and George had gone to get a pop. They were taking their sweet time, fishing through the cooler and plucking bags of chips off the rack, as if they owned the place. No one cared two hoots about what they were doing or what was going on until Johnny Flowers walked in. Dave could remember it as clearly as if it had happened yesterday. Old Angus nudging his daughter; Elizabeth coming out from behind the counter and watching Johnny's every move. It was true. Whenever anything went wrong at school, everyone suspected Johnny Flowers.

"By the time I was in grade four," said Johnny, "I used to head for the office at the end of the day to serve detention, whether I had one or not."

"So what happened to you?" asked Dave.

"My dad got a job out west," said Johnny.

They left town the autumn he turned eleven.

They drove west in the Thunderbird. Just the two of them.

It took them a week to get across the country. And the further they got from Cape Breton, the freer Johnny felt.

On his first day at his new school, he stood in the schoolyard and cased out all the kids. Girls with books in their arms, boys tossing balls. He realized not one solitary soul knew him. And he wasn't scared.

"It made me happy," he said. "On the way into class, I ducked into the boys' room and threw away the pack of chew I had just bought."

They were both silent for a moment.

Then Johnny said, "How'd you find me anyway?"

Dave told him about finding the centennial mug in the second-hand store in Bridgewater. And how he wanted to give it back, how he tracked him down. Johnny laughed. "Centennial baby," he said. "The summer before we went west, there was a big headline in the newspaper. 'Centennial Baby Sets Fire to Patterson's Woodshed.' Do you remember that? That was an accident, man. And it wasn't me. Someone should ask Jimmy Patterson about that fire. Jimmy Patterson was the one what did it. Anyway. I don't know anything about that mug. And I don't want it."

Dave reached out and took the silver mug from Kenny and put it back in the lacquered box.

"That's the whole story," said Dave.

"Sounds like a hard-knock life," said Kenny.

"No, no," said Dave. "He was good. He is an engineer, of all things. Or working for an engineering firm or something. I liked him, anyway."

"But he didn't want the mug."

"No," said Dave.

"And that bugs you, doesn't it?" said Kenny.

"I guess," said Dave.

Dave refilled Kenny's coffee, and they sat there for a while staring out the front window of his store, at the people outside, their shoulders hunched against the rain.

In the end, Dave kept the mug for a year. He left it right on the counter of the store. Soon enough it faded into the background, but never completely from his mind. He considered sending it to Annie for her birthday.

It would have been funny. But it didn't feel right.

And then one autumn afternoon, when he was looking for his cheque book, he came across the Johnny Flowers notebook. He sat down and read it through. Front to back. That night he wrote a letter to an old friend in Big Narrows. In the letter he posed a question. It was a month before he got an answer.

It came from Russell Montgomery, Big Narrows's ancient librarian and unofficial historian.

David, his letter began,

> *We would love to have the mug. And anything*
> *else you might have from those days. We will ask*
> *others too, and if we gather a few things of interest*
> *we will put together a display of that wonderful*
> *summer. So hard to believe our 100th birthday*
> *was so many summers ago. My goodness, we are*
> *almost halfway to the next.*

Dave folded the letter and slipped it back into its envelope.

Those boyhood days he had spent in the Narrows were fading faster and faster down the mysterious alley of yesterday. For some reason he didn't fully understand, he needed someone to acknowledge that they had mattered. That they were important days. Johnny Flowers hadn't offered him the reassurance he was looking for. Dave's important yesterdays weren't Johnny's. You can't choose who is going to guard your history.

He spent an hour or so one afternoon up in the storage room over his store and assembled a little pile of stuff. An old blue and orange felt pennant with the name of the town. The jacket he had worn in the school band. His green knitted cub jersey, with a complete set of badges and two yellow arm stripes. He folded them all up carefully, and put them in a box with some newspaper clippings from that centennial summer. He set the mug in the middle of it all, like an egg in a nest. The idea of it landing on a shelf in the little town museum made him happy. The mug would be there for years, maybe even after he was gone. If it was lucky, it would be pulled out during the celebrations of the town's *second* century. Maybe, even, presented again. Dave sealed his box of memories and addressed it carefully.

God bless Russell Montgomery, and all those librarians and amateur historians, those soldiers of the past who believe in stories, no matter whose stories they are. While we hold onto our little lives, they hold onto all of them—keepers of the collective past.

The mug didn't belong to Dave, or to Johnny Flowers, anymore. The story of how Dave dropped Johnny and how both he and Johnny had ended up leaving town would soon be forgotten. Here is what would remain. There was a summer long ago, and a baby, and a silver mug. And it really happened, and it did matter.

ATTACK OF THE TREADMILL

In the name of God, help me.
—DAVE

Beginnings are always the hardest.

The writer beginning a story is like a butterfly in a garden, sometimes starting with a rush, flitting from leaf to leaf, barely landing here before he flutters there. Other times, he's frozen, a pen hovering over the page without one single idea. The little butterfly of the mind is overwhelmed by the confusion of possibility until, unbidden, the warm wind of inspiration begins to blow, and the little wings begin to pump, so faintly he doesn't notice at first. Then he catches movement out of the corner of his mind's eye and he knows that at any moment, he will lift off, and the story will begin.

This story began the Saturday morning Dave's shoelace broke.

It began like this.

Dave and Morley were on their way to the market. The idea was to go early and get back before Sam woke up. The idea was fresh blueberry pancakes for breakfast.

They were running late, of course. Morley was at least three steps ahead of Dave. He could sense her frustration beginning to simmer. He was hurrying to catch up, trying to make it to the door before the simmer became a boil.

He thought he was ready, but of course, he wasn't close to ready. He had to run upstairs for his wallet, and then, after he had done that, he couldn't find the car keys, anywhere. He looked at his wife, grinned awkwardly and said, "I'm sure I left them here." He was pointing at the basket by the back door.

Of course he hadn't left them in the basket by the back door. They could both see that. And if you knew him, you could tell by the way he said *I am sure I left them here* that he *wasn't* sure at all, that he didn't have a clue where he had left them. Anyway, he had checked the basket five minutes ago.

The keys, it turns out, were upstairs, in the laundry basket, in the pocket of the jeans he was wearing on Thursday, which was the last time he drove the car. That only took ten minutes to work out.

Morley was waiting by the door through all this—through the discovery that the keys *were* missing, and the searching, and the working out. She was waiting still when he came triumphantly down the stairs with the keys in hand.

"I have no idea what they were doing *there*," he said, genuinely mystified. And he stepped into his sneakers and sat on the stairs to do them up.

"Go on," he said to Morley. As if she hadn't been waiting since this began.

"I'll be right out," he said. And he pulled the lace on the left shoe and the lace snapped.

And *that* is the moment this story began—that moment by the back door when Dave's shoelace broke, and Dave said "Just a minute," and ran to the basement. He grabbed the first thing he saw that had laces, which was a pair of skates. He ripped out the long waxed lace from one of the skates, stuffed it in his pocket and tripped out to the car, his shoe half on and half off.

When they got to the market, Dave headed for a little café by the entrance.

"I'll catch up," he said. And he sat there and threaded the skate lace into his sneaker.

When he was finished, there was a lot of lace left over. So he did a double knot and stuffed the leftover lace into the shoe, and he was good to go.

Sam was awake when they got home, but it was Saturday, and he was watching television, not even close to feeding himself, so technically they made it in time. They had the pancakes for *lunch.*

Two weeks went by. It was a Friday, twilight. That sweet moment of indifference between day and night.

Dave and Morley, with Sam in the back seat, were in the sweetest place you can be for that great cosmic sigh. They were on the road, between here and there, trying to decide where they were going to pull off the highway for the night.

"I don't care," said Sam, "as long as it has a pool."

They were in upstate New York, on a spur-of-the-moment road trip. They had dipped across the border because it seemed like fun, like the old days. They had no destination, nowhere to be except on Sunday evening. On the way home, they were going to stop to have supper with Stephanie and her boyfriend, Tommy.

Up ahead, on the edge of one of those little highway towns that you have never heard of, there was a motel with a big *vacancy* sign lit up. Blue and green neon flickering against the purple sky.

Dave slowed down. "Check it out," he said.

There was another sign.

Sam gasped. And began to read the sign out loud.

"Indoor ..."

Morley cut him off and finished his sentence. "Pool," she said. "It means pool ... indoor *pool*. The *l* has burnt out."

Sam said, "Can we take a picture?"

The Totem Motor Inn. Indoor pool. Dave pulled off the road.

Before long, Morley was settling onto the chaise longue on their second-floor balcony with her book. Sam had flounced onto the bed with the TV remote.

"Sweet," he said. "Satellite."

"Come on," said Dave. Five minutes later, Dave and Sam were heading for the pool.

There was another kid in the water. He was about the same age as Sam. Maybe a little younger. He was acting a little younger.

Dave stood on the concrete deck watching the kid struggle out of the shallow end. He was feeling sorry for the boy and angry at his absent parents. Then the kid walked right up to Dave and, without a word, jumped into the water, clutching his knees to his stomach.

Cannonball!

"Hey," said Dave, jumping back. Too late. The kid swam underwater to the other side of the pool.

Sam looked at him and said, "Do you want to play Marco Polo?"

The kid said, "Marco Polo is for babies."

He was loud and splashy. He was obnoxious. He ruined their swim.

Dave lingered behind as Sam headed back to their room. As soon as Sam was out of earshot, Dave leaned over to the kid and said, "You should know better."

The next morning, Dave woke up first. He lay in bed for a while, waiting, but Morley wasn't stirring, and Sam was out cold on the bed by the window.

After a few minutes, he propped himself on his elbow and whispered in his sleeping wife's ear, "I am going to go have a walk about. I'll bring you a coffee."

Morley mumbled, "Don't hurry," and rolled over.

Dave pulled on the pants and shirt he was wearing the night before and padded to the door. He hung the *do not disturb* sign on the handle and closed the door softly behind him.

There is something about a Saturday morning in September, something about the quality of the air and light, that makes September Saturdays among the sweetest days of the year.

When he was a boy, Dave believed it was because school was closed on Saturdays—teachers and supply cupboards safely out of reach, the air of anxiety under lock and key.

But why now? After all these school-less years? It seemed more certain than an echo.

It could be the tipping of the world, the sad old story of the sun slipping away, summer slipping away with it, winter coming over the hills.

Or maybe it's the farmers. The autumn farmers, who get up

before the Saturday sun, load their trucks and then haul their berries and bushels of corn to all the little farmers' markets in all the towns and cities. The farmers setting off some sort of autumnal vibration wherever they pass.

Whatever it is, September Saturdays make Dave feel like a boy. On Saturdays in September, Dave still wants to be first out to play.

He took the stairs two at a time.

There was a girl behind the desk wearing a brown tunic.

"Morning," she said, with a cheery Saturday smile. She pointed down the hall.

"Complimentary breakfast in the Crockett Room."

"Not yet," said Dave. Then he reconsidered. "Maybe coffee."

She said, "Coffee's complimentary. All you can drink."

Dave was thinking he'd get a coffee to go, walk into town and buy a paper. Maybe they'd have *The Times*. Maybe he could find a place in town that had waffles or something.

"Boone's is good," said the girl.

Dave set off, past the stairs and the rack with all the brochures, past the dark bar where he and Morley had had a beer by the fireplace after supper, past the pool. He made a right turn after the fitness centre, and there was the Crockett Room.

He had to use his room key to open the fitness centre door.

He went in backwards, pushing the door with his hip, coffee in one hand and a surprisingly delicious cinnamon bun in the other.

The room was bigger than you would have expected, but

small nonetheless. Some free weights. A stair climber. And one of those, whatever you call them, running machines with the black belts. He had never tried one. And he wasn't about to try one now.

He glanced at his watch.

Except it *was* early. And no one else was around.

There was just him and the girl in the tunic, and she was at the desk.

He had always wondered what they were like, these machines. Would there ever be a better time to find out? A Saturday in September?

It was curiosity, mostly. Although, truth be told, Dave had been thinking he should join a gym, start working out, maybe in the mornings before he opened the store, or at lunch. Or right now. *Carpe diem.*

He climbed tentatively onto the black treadmill. That's what they called them. Treadmills. He took a tentative hop. It had a pleasing spring.

He balanced his coffee on the arm and stared at the thing.

There was an LED control panel with a daunting number of choices. *Age, Weight, Aerobic, Anaerobic, Fitness level.* Fitness level? What were his choices? Couch potato? Slug?

They made these things unnecessarily complicated, thought Dave. They should just have *On* and *Off*.

Dave picked up his coffee and took a sip. He stared at the screen.

Personalized Program. That was promising.

He pressed *Personalized Program.*

A voice said, "Good morning ... Brendan. Are you ready to rock?"

And then the belt Dave was standing on lurched, and he was almost catapulted off the end. What was left of his coffee flew out of his hand and splashed onto the display panel.

The belt was moving, so Dave was, too. Not exactly running, not even jogging, but not walking either—somewhere between walking and running, keeping up with the belt.

And the voice, which Dave now realized was coming *out* of the machine, was saying "… in ten, nine, eight … "

Much too much was happening, and it was happening much too quickly. The treadmill was moving a little faster than was comfortable. Dave was puffing a bit and scanning the control panel as he puffed. He was looking for the *Off* button. *There must be one.* Suddenly he lurched forward, almost falling, regaining his balance at the last moment. It felt like someone had grabbed his left foot. He looked down. Both ends of the overlong hockey lace were disappearing into the bowels of the machine.

His shoelace was wrapping itself around the treadmill rollers. He couldn't pull it loose. It was all he could do to keep even more of it from disappearing. He was trapped.

And then the voice from the machine was saying "… two, one."

There was a flourish of trumpets; maybe it was the theme from *Rocky*. He couldn't be sure about that; he couldn't be sure about anything frankly, except the voice, which said, "Hit it, Brendan!" The treadmill sped up, and Dave was off and running for his life now.

"Hey!" he said.

But no one was listening.

If the treadmill had been listening, it wouldn't have begun to rise into the air the way it did. Not the entire mechanism—just the belt. So Dave was now running uphill.

His heart was pounding, his legs were pumping, his mind was racing. Just who was this Brendan, and why on earth would he choose to do this to himself?

And then Dave felt a wave of relief. There *was* an *Off* button— right in front of him as plain as day. He smiled and pressed it. And nothing happened.

He pressed it again. The machine gave a little shudder and then picked up speed. Brendan's personalized training program was shifting into another gear. Dave, in desperation, began pounding on the button, then on the rest of the panel. He was smashing it with his hand, pounding on all the buttons, but nothing he did seemed to have any effect whatsoever.

That's what happens when you soak a solid-state circuit board in coffee. But Dave didn't know that. And that's not all he didn't know.

He didn't know, for instance, that the mysterious Brendan, who had carelessly left his flash drive in the preferences port, was training for the Boston Marathon. Or that he was about to re-experience Brendan's last training session—a simulated twenty-three-kilometre run through the Adirondack Mountains.

All Dave knew was that he could feel the belt under his feet speeding up. And the incline rising in front of him. All Dave knew was that he was *literally* running for his life.

He was running through the mountains with his left foot in a leghold trap.

As he stormed along, he was staring at a big red and white wall poster.

Start out slowly, said the poster. *Talk to your doctor before exercising.*

Dave pounded along for twelve minutes until he couldn't pound anymore. He managed to get his right foot onto the side platform. He had to leave his left foot behind.

He stood there catching his breath, his free foot on the side platform and his trapped foot chugging away on the treadmill like the piston of some ancient machine.

Desperate times require desperate measures. Dave bent down and grabbed the edges of the rubber treadmill belt with his hands. He actually managed to stop it for an instant. There was a squeal and the sound of gears grinding. There was smoke and a searing pain in Dave's hands. He could feel the treadmill's pent-up energy building. It was more than he could fight, but he kept holding on, because what else could he do? There was a bang, and he was catapulted back onto the belt. He landed backwards.

He was running backwards now, up an Adirondack mountain, faster than he had ever run forward in his life.

His calves were burning, and sweat was pouring from every pore of his body.

And the voice on the machine said, "Let's take it up a notch, Brendan."

In desperation Dave leapt in the air and spun around. He was facing forward again, pawing at the buttons on his shirt as he ran. He ripped his shirt off and threw it on the ground. Bare chested, sweaty and red, Dave ran, his fists pumping back and forth. He couldn't keep this up much longer.

That's when he spotted the plug.

Of course, what a fool, all he had to do was pull out the plug and this whole horrible thing would stop.

The cord came out the front of the machine and snaked around to the right. If he was lucky, maybe he could lean out, and grab it, and pull it out of the wall. He was running, and bending, and stretching. He almost had it. Just an inch or two more and—ohmigod, he was losing his balance. His arms were windmilling the air. He was going down.

Before you could say—well, any number of things come to mind; they came to Dave's mind—before you could say any of those things, Dave was sitting on the treadmill, bouncing along on his bum, riding it like a kid on a toboggan.

You may think this sounds funny—but it wasn't funny at all. Imagine, if you will, how a man, a man in the prime of his life, a man of dignity, a man of substance, a man of accomplishments, a man with a standing in his community ... okay, never mind— just imagine Dave, poor Dave, his life about to be cut short because he was going to lose a heroic battle with a piece of fitness equipment. It's *not* funny. And it became even less funny when he tried to get up. He tried to get up. But all he had the strength to do was lift himself onto his hands and knees.

Now he was crawling through the mountains in double, triple, quadruple time, scrabbling faster than he would have believed possible, like a video in fast forward.

And that is when the fitness room door opened.

"In the name of God," croaked Dave, "help me."

And he looked over his shoulder—right into the eyes of the kid from the swimming pool.

"The plug," gasped Dave. "Pull the plug."

The kid from the swimming pool was eating an ice-cream bar. He stood there licking his ice cream like he was watching a parade.

He shook his head. "You should know better," he said.

And he turned around and walked out of the room.

Dave kept crawling for another ten minutes. He managed to get himself back onto his feet. He made his peace with God and the fates. He should have guessed he would die like this. Not the dignified exit he had hoped for. He would fall again, and his whole body would get sucked into the roller and he would be flattened like some sort of cartoon character.

That is what he was thinking when the fitness door opened again and someone said, "Hey, man. I think I left my flash drive in your machine."

Dave tried to summon as much dignity as he could.

"Whatever," said Dave. "I was just finishing. It's all yours."

Brendan, maybe twenty-five or twenty-seven, certainly not thirty, reached out, flipped up a plastic cover on the control panel, and removed his drive. The machine stopped abruptly.

Dave, unfortunately, kept running. He cracked into the control panel and landed in a heap at Brendan's feet.

"You okay, man?" asked Brendan.

It was barely nine-thirty when Dave got back to the room.

Morley was sitting on the bed surrounded by brochures. Sam was in his swim trunks.

"Hey," said Sam, as Dave fell onto the bed, lay on his back, and stared at the ceiling.

"Hey," said Dave.

Endings are no easier for a writer. Where, for instance, do we end this?

With Dave, stiff, and sore, and bruised, limping down to the pool for a game of Marco Polo with Sam? Or with him struggling through a pine-scented forest beside his wife, praying a mountain lion finishes him off before he has to continue any further down the trail? Or maybe with the long, aching ride home, Morley behind the wheel, Dave reclining in the passenger seat, his legs covered by the bags of ice he has bought at a roadside gas station, his rubber-burned hands slathered in ointment?

Or maybe here, in the hotel room. With Morley cheerfully marking off hiking routes on the map she has found on her bedside table, Sam excitedly pulling on his still-damp swim trunks, and Dave on the bed, groaning softly—a Saturday in September, sunny and promising, stretching out before them like a white line down the middle of a country road.

GABRIEL DUBOIS

And that is when the goat walked into the kitchen."
—DAVE

The branch came down one night that spring. No one saw it happen. Someone could have been killed if it had happened in the day—that's what everyone said. By breakfast, half the neighbourhood had been over to take a look. It was lying half on Jim Scoffield's front lawn and half on the street, as thick around as your thigh where it snapped off. It missed Jim's fence and the Chudarys' car—but just. By noon, the city had come, and gone, and all that was left were some leaves in the gutter and a few small branches on Jim's lawn. No harm done. But that wasn't the end of it, of course.

The next week, some guys arrived with drills and clipboards and poked around for over an hour. Everyone knew the tree's number was up.

It was a magnificent tree. A maple. And for as long as anyone could remember, it had arched over Jim's corner lot with the benevolence of a sermon. It had something to offer every season: in the spring, the rainfall of flowers, the excitement of seeds; in summer, the benediction of shade—you could feel the temperature drop as you walked under its graceful shadow. But best of all, in the autumn, its red glory. Jim's maple tree sang its way through the years, but now it would be singing no more.

It took the crew from the city a day to bring it down, buzzing around the branches like hornets with their mechanical crane and chainsaws. Sam saw them arrive in the morning, and he kept returning to the living-room window all day, a forlorn witness. By the time Dave came home, both the truck and the tree were gone.

"You'd think it would take longer," said Dave. "Like a week or something."

But it took a day. They came and they carted it away and that was that. A hundred, a hundred and fifty years … gone.

The corner looked barren.

Sam looked bereft.

After supper, Dave said, "Let's go check on Jim."

What he meant was, let's check the hole on Jim's lawn.

Jim was sitting on his front porch. He was looking at a brochure.

The man in charge told him they would be back with a replacement tree. He said Jim could choose what kind. Jim held up the brochure. He had three choices. He could have a honey locust, a gingko or a little-leaf linden.

"Why not a maple?" asked Dave. "They should plant a maple."

"They want *smaller* trees," said Jim. "So they don't get in the wires, or, you know"—he waved his hand around his yard—"come down in storms." Jim didn't sound happy.

"Or have kids climbing in them," said Sam.

They were quiet for a few minutes, sitting there squinting at the evening sun and the space where the tree had been.

Dave was the first to say something.

Dave said, "Can you tell them not to plant anything?"

Jim said, "What?"

Dave said, "Tell them to leave the place alone. I have an idea."

When they got home, Sam said, "What is your idea?"

Dave sat down on the front stoop. He patted the stair beside him.

Dave grew up with trees. He grew up with trees all around him. On the mountains and the woodlots and the leaf-shaded streets of Big Narrows. But just as fish don't notice the water they swim in, Dave never noticed the trees—until the summer he was eleven, the summer he met Gabriel Dubois. That was the summer he went to the Dubois farm with Billy Mitchell, who was twelve and who had been to the old man's place before with his big brother.

Dubois's place was in the hills on the far side of Macaulay's farm.

"If we take him crabapples," said Billy, "he will pay us."

Billy knew a crabapple tree that grew along the fence line at the back of Macaulay's. They left their bikes in the graveyard and followed the fence in. They had an old rucksack they filled with the apples and took turns carrying it, up the mountain road, to the blueberry field, where they stopped and rested.

As they sprawled there, sweaty under the August sun, Dave pulled an apple from the bag and held it, all red, waxy and perfectly sweet smelling. He shook his head and then bit into it. He spat the mouthful out with a groan. It was maybe the tenth one he had tried.

"How can they *look* so good," he said.

When Billy didn't answer he asked, "Why does he want them, anyway?"

"Makes jam," said Billy, who was on his way again. "Come on."

Actually, it was jelly he made. Crabapple *jelly*. Although he hadn't made it for years, because it wasn't him who made it, but his wife. And by that summer, Ellen Dubois had been dead a decade. Maybe more.

It's not that he *couldn't* have made it. He had all her formulas, as he called them. They were written in a school scribbler with a picture of a dog wearing a gingham apron on the cover. He wasn't helpless or shy in the kitchen. He didn't make it because he didn't need it. He had a cellar full of the stuff. Shelves and shelves of his wife's jellies and jams that she had left behind her. All of the jars meticulously dated. He was working through the basement in order. But he was falling behind, getting through only one year of her production for every three years that passed. There was no way he was going to finish in a lifetime.

He would pay any boys who brought him apples nonetheless. He had his reputation to maintain. And besides, he liked the idea of boys messing around in trees. He liked it when they showed up with their bags full of apples.

"Come on," said Billy.

He helped Dave put on the rucksack and then tramped off to the far corner of the field, where he stepped around a big maple and slipped out of sight, onto a path Dave didn't know existed.

"Come on," he called again.

Dave looked back over his shoulder, and then hustled to catch up.

Almost immediately they were walking downhill—down through the quiet, cool forest, past the large rocks and through a ravine. After a while, the path levelled, wound through a stand of cedars and then skirted a tamarack swamp. The ground was spongy from the beavers who lived there before the boys were born, back when Ellen Dubois was putting up her jams and jellies. On the far side of the swamp, they started up again, through the pines and the stands of birch and maple, into the back hills.

They came out on the edge of an overgrown field, the grass up to their waists, crickets flying all around. There was a house on the far side, paint all peeling. And a grey shed, a fading barn.

Billy said, "*Come on.*"

Dave said, "Are you sure?"

It was spooky, coming out of the woods like that and finding the place, no road or anything. But Dave had come this far. So he followed Billy, brushing his hand along the top of the grass. He pulled out a stalk of timothy, stuck the sweet pale end of it in his mouth and chewed it nervously.

They found the old man behind the shed. He was wearing a faded green work shirt, matching work pants, suspenders, and leather boots, untied.

He was splitting wood. There were logs scattered around him.

"We brought you crabapples, Mr. Dubois," said Billy.

The old man was unshaven and sweaty. He took the bag and pulled out an apple. He bit into it.

Dave was holding his breath.

Mr. Dubois actually swallowed.

"*Eh bien*," he said. "From the tree by the old fence back of Macaulay's."

Billy looked at Dave. *See, I told you.*

They stood on the porch, peering into the kitchen, while the old man rummaged around, opening cupboards and drawers. When he found what he was looking for, a slab of something wrapped in cheesecloth, he carried it to the kitchen table. It looked like a brick of plastic, about the size of an encyclopedia. He got a hammer from under the sink and hit the plastic with the hammer. A piece broke off.

He hit it again. He handed each boy fifty cents and a piece of the plastic-looking stuff.

"For the walk back," he said.

"And that," said Dave, "is when the goat walked into the kitchen."

Dave and Sam were still sitting on the front stoop. Sam had half a Popsicle in his hand. Little red drops were pooling on the ground in front of him.

Sam said, "A goat?"

"It had been in the living room, watching TV. He told us the goat was sick. He said he was nursing it. The old man told us the goat's name was Estelle.

"So we said hi to the goat," said Dave. "And then we left."

"What was it he gave you?" asked Sam. "The thing he broke with the hammer?"

"Homemade spruce gum," said Dave.

"You had to work at it to get it going," said Dave. "It was brittle. So it crumbled. You had to hold it in your mouth and work up your saliva and work it together. I didn't like it at first. It's not like store-bought gum. It's not sweet."

"What does it taste like?" said Sam.

"It tastes like the forest," said Dave. "Like trees."

"Could you blow bubbles?" said Sam.

"I don't know," said Dave. "I forget. But I remember it *was* pink like bubble gum and it tasted like the forest. Like a forest in the spring with lots of birds."

Dave went on about the gum for some time. About how Gabriel Dubois would go out in the winter with a chisel attached to the end of a long pole and collect the hard sap bubbles from the spruce trees. How he would take it home, put it in his sap bucket, melt it down and pick out the little bits of bark. How he would strain the sticky liquid through cheesecloth and let it set in a tin pan. When the sap hardened up, he would break it into pieces and dust them in cornstarch. Then he would wrap the pieces in wax paper and take them to MacDonnell's store. You could buy a piece for two pennies.

"You remember that?" said Sam.

"Well, truthfully," said Dave, "he wasn't doing that when I was a boy. That was from my dad's time. But he was still making it.

"He was the real deal. No one knew the forest like Gabriel Dubois."

That's what Dave's dad, Charlie, had said that night when Dave told him they had been to his place.

"We sold him crabapples," said Dave.

Charlie smiled and said, "Did he give you any spruce gum?"

Dave leaned back onto the stairs and pointed over at Jim's yard. "It is so strange with the tree gone," he said.

Sam said, "Is Mr. Dubois the guy with the exploding tree?"

"Ah," said Dave. "I was coming to that one. I forgot I had told you that one already. I shouldn't have ever *told* you that one. I should have showed you."

"Just tell it," said Sam. "I like that one."

"Well," said Dave. "It was the next summer. We used to hike all around."

Sam nodded.

Dave said, "We would see him sometimes."

"Where?" said Sam.

"All around," said Dave. "In the woods, I mean. Anyway, one day we were down by the swamp, digging."

"For what?" asked Sam.

"For water," said Dave. "The ground is all spongy down there. We thought maybe there was a buried lake ... And he showed up. And he started to—"

"Wait a minute. Wait a minute," said Sam. "You would be in the woods, and he would show up. And you would talk to him."

Dave said, "Yeah."

"That is just creepy," said Sam. "You wouldn't let me do any of this."

They did see Mr. Dubois a lot that summer. He was like a new word. *Gabriel.* You live your whole life and never notice it, ever, and then one day you read it somewhere, and you look up the meaning in the dictionary, and once you do that ... *poof*, you come across it everywhere. Like it was there all the time, except until you knew what it meant, you were blind to it.

They met him by the creek, by the swamp and at the trouting pond.

"At the pond where we fished last summer?" asked Sam.

"Right there," said Dave. "On the mountain. We'd go swimming—"

"You'd be swimming?" said Sam, interrupting.

"What's wrong with that?" said Dave.

"First off," said Sam. "There were no lifeguards."

"That's right," said Dave.

"Second off," said Sam. "He was a stranger. And he gave you candy."

"Well, gum," said Dave. "But only once or twice. Mostly he gave us nuts."

"Same difference," said Sam.

"Now wait a minute," said Dave. "He wasn't *technically* a stranger. We saw him lots."

"In the woods," said Sam. "You would *freak out* if I told you I met a man in the woods who gave me candy."

"You have a point," said Dave.

Sam said, "Whatever."

Dave said, "Anyway, if you will let me continue, we were down by the swamp, and he came out of the woods—that was another thing about him, he never walked on the paths or anything. He would walk right through the forest. And he'd stop and talk to us, you know, say hi, or whatever, and that day as he walked away, he took his axe—"

Sam said, "He had an axe?"

"He *always* had an axe," said Dave.

"Bro-*ther*."

"Anyway," said Dave. "The point is, as he walked away, he walked by a birch tree. He goes by it, then he stops, and turns around and looks at it, and he shakes his head, like he doesn't want to do what he is going to do next. But he does it anyway. He stops, and puts his axe down. This is a big birch tree, right? Like a full-grown tree. And then he swings at the tree with his bare fist, and when he hits it—"

"The tree explodes," said Sam.

"That's right," said Dave.

There were three of them there that afternoon, and they all saw it happen. Billy Mitchell, Gordy Beaman and Dave. You could ask any of them. They would tell you the exactly same thing.

Gabriel Dubois wound up, punched the tree, and the tree exploded.

"With his bare fist?" said Sam.

"With his bare fist," said Dave.

Now, Billy, Gordy and Dave, none of them said a word. They just stared with their mouths hanging open while he walked away. When he was out of sight, Billy Mitchell said, "Did you see that?"

What had happened was not only impossible, it was beyond belief. The tree *actually* exploded. Gabriel Dubois hit the tree, and there was a sound like, like *woooof*. And then a burst of smoke, and the tree was gone. It vanished into thin air.

"It was like a movie," said Dave.

Sam said, "Was it a big tree?"

"It was a huge tree," said Dave. "A huge tree."

They went over, to see it, like they were sneaking up on an animal that might have been dead, but also might have been alive. Which is to say, they were careful going up to it.

And when they got there ...

"It *was* gone," said Dave. "There was nothing left of it."

"Nothing?" said Sam.

"There was a pile of sawdust," said Dave, "and bark. Like a hollow tube of bark. Like the skin. Of course, you know what happened then?"

"Yep," said Sam.

"We pulled straws," said Dave. "Billy won."

"Won?" said Sam.

"Well," said Dave. "I don't know."

They pulled straws, and Billy got the short one. They found a birch that looked the same size; it looked *exactly* the same. Billy took his shirt off and wrapped it around his fist.

"He was a pretty determined kid," said Dave "You have to give him that."

"What happened?" said Sam.

"He broke his knuckles in four places," said Dave.

That's how they learned about yellow birches.

That's how they learned that when a yellow birch dies, it doesn't fall over, but stands straight and tall, and rots from the inside, until all that remains of it is a tube of birchbark standing there *looking* like a tree. Looking like a tree and just waiting for someone with a crowd of boys to amaze.

"It was all about choosing the right tree," said Dave. "But it took us a while to figure that out."

"I don't see what any of this has to do with your plan for Jim's yard," said Sam.

"I'm coming to that," said Dave. And he stood up and went into the kitchen.

"What I am trying to explain here is that Gabriel Dubois knew everything there was to know about trees. He used to make maple syrup every year. Now, lots of people in the Narrows used to do that. The Macaulays still do. And they make good syrup, don't get me wrong. That is the syrup we get every year. But they make it from *sugar* maples. That sugar bush we walk through on the way to the pond in the summer, that's the Macaulays', and that is a good maple bush. It is on the south side of the mountain, like you'd want. But those are *sugar* maples. And sugar maples are what everyone taps.

"Gabriel Dubois used to tap *silver* maples.

"And the syrup he made ... well ... I wish you could try some. It was so light and sweet. It was like heaven. He used to put it up in glass jam jars."

"Why doesn't everyone use silver maples?" Sam asked.

"Because you can't make enough. So you can't make money. There isn't as much sap. But he didn't care about that. He used wooden buckets and beechwood taps, and when he collected the sap, he made the syrup the Native way. They didn't have pots. So they couldn't boil it. Did you ever think of that? You know how they did it?"

Sam shook his head.

Dave said, "They let it freeze up and then they skimmed off the ice ... over and over ... so it got concentrated. And that way, it never tasted burnt.

"Not many people in Big Narrows ever got to try his stuff."

"Why?" said Sam.

"Because it all went to a fancy hotel in Halifax. They would come every year and pick it up."

"But you did," said Sam.

"That's right," said Dave. "But only when I was older and moved away.

"He was quite a guy," said Dave. "He made all sorts of stuff. Made toilet water from witch hazel. They sold it in the drugstore in Baddeck."

"Toilet water?" said Sam.

"Aftershave," said Dave. "And cough medicine from wild cherry trees. He sold it to the doctor. When I was a kid, that's what they would give you when you were sick. Gabriel Dubois's cough syrup. True fact."

Dave had been talking for over an hour. All about Gabriel Dubois. Dead and gone now, what? Twenty-five years?

And now he was rummaging through the fridge. Sam was sitting at the kitchen table. The floor around the fridge was littered with food—jars of jam, hunks of cheese, half a leftover chicken, a jug of orange juice. Dave was leaning into the fridge, wrestling with something buried in the back. Finally, he backed out and held up a dented cookie tin. "Aha!" he said.

"What is it?" asked Sam.

Dave put the tin down on the table.

Sam reached for it, but Dave shook his head.

Dave said, "Just a minute. I am nearly finished."

Dave said, "Before I was born, there used to be men who travelled the countryside looking for wood. This was after the first growth was gone. They were hardwood buyers. If they found a good tree on your property, like black walnut say, or a cherry tree—they always liked cherrywood, cherrywood got scarce pretty quick—they would pay you to let them take it down."

Now, in Big Narrows, there happened to be a little stand of cherry trees right on the lawn in front of the library. And finally one of those buyers made it to town. He almost got them all for five hundred bucks. Council had approved the sale and it was going to happen—until Gabriel heard about it and came to town and told them the trees were worth more than the library. He put a stop to that.

Dave said, "Next time we go to Grandma's, look out my bedroom window, my old bedroom upstairs, and look down towards town. You'll see how pretty looking it is, all those trees, the town sort of nestled there in the trees, the way the clock tower pokes through them, and how, when you are in town, the light pokes through the leaves. That is because of Gabriel Dubois."

"But what's in the box?" said Sam again.

"Well okay," said Dave. "I am getting to that.

"There was this big oak that belonged to old Mr. Nettleship. I guess it was on the lawn in front of his store, this is a long time ago. This is before I was born, I never saw the store. The store burned down before I was born. And when it did, Mr. Nettleship built further down the street, near the bridge, where the hardware is today. The plan was to widen the street where his old store was, and to do that, they were going to take down the oak.

"But when the day came to take it down, Gabriel Dubois was sitting at the bottom of the tree. The way they tell it, he was tipped back on a kitchen chair he got from the Maple Leaf Restaurant.

"And he wouldn't let them do it. He said the tree had been there maybe three, four hundred years, and no road was that important.

"He said, 'Cars have wheels, they can go around it.'

"He saved the tree. And they started calling it Gabby's oak. And eventually they put a little bench under it and they called it Gabby's. People used to say, 'I'll meet you at Gabby's,' and they meant the bench under the oak tree.

"He was right, of course. The cars went around it, no problem.

"Well, it turned out it was the biggest oak for miles. Maybe on all of Cape Breton as far as I know.

"After the big flood in 1954, the mayor nailed a yardstick on it and marked the spot where the water stopped. People would check it every year. Our hockey team never won anything, but we had the biggest tree around.

"And if Gabby Dubois was right, that tree must be five hundred years old now."

Dave sat down at the table. He was struggling with the box, with the tin lid.

He said, "An oak tree needs help getting its seeds around. They are too heavy to blow in the wind, the way maple keys do. They just fall straight down, and there is not a lot of room under a five-hundred-year-old oak tree for another one to grow."

Dave had the lid off the box now. He handed it to Sam. Sam peered in.

"Acorns?" he said.

"Yep," said Dave. The tin was filled with small plastic bags, each holding a dozen or so acorns.

"From Gabby's tree. I brought them back a few years ago. I had an idea that I would mail a couple of them to everyone who ever lived in Big Narrows. I wanted to have a hundred of Gabby's oaks growing all over the country."

"But you didn't do it," said Sam.

"Well," said Dave. "I *haven't* done it. Not yet."

The next day, before breakfast, Dave and Sam headed over to Jim's. They were carrying a spade, and a watering can, and the cookie tin.

When they were finished, Sam emptied the watering can on the freshly turned soil. Then he picked up the tin of acorns and gave it a gentle shake. The acorns made a pleasing rattle. "Gabby's oaks," said Sam.

He looked at his father and held up the tin.

"Gabby's oaks," said Dave.

They both smiled.

"Well," said Sam. "Where to next?"

CODE YELLOW

You call for me. Tell her there was an accident. Tell her I am in a coma.
     —DAVE

Morning. But—an unhurried morning. Dave and Morley are in their kitchen, both of them getting ready for the day ahead, when Dave says, "I am going to visit Marty in the hospital."

Morley, who has her back to him, turns with eyebrows arched.

"Really?" she says.

"Come on," said Dave. "That's not fair."

Wasn't it? Dave's relationship with hospitals over the years has not been, well … without problems. Why, the very first time Dave and Morley were in a hospital together Dave had fainted, flat cold.

It was a week or so before Stephanie was born. They had gone with their birthing class. The big tour.

And halfway through the tour, when they were led into the actual *birthing room,* and Dave came face to face with the moment of truth, with the birthing *table*, his knees had buckled, and he had staggered against the green concrete wall.

Three of the other fathers picked him up, carried him across the room and laid him out on the table.

It was Ron, the class clown, who had put Dave's feet into the stirrups.

"Come on," said Dave. "That was over twenty years ago."

"What?" said Morley. "Things have changed since then?"

It isn't that Dave is a full-blown hypochondriac. Morley would never say that. He isn't. But there is no denying he has hypochondriacal tendencies. And those tendencies, mixed with his ... well ... his personality, tend to get him in trouble.

There was, for instance, the time he inhaled the fly. He became convinced that the fly was alive in his lungs, was colonizing his lungs. We know this because Dave's friend Kenny Wong caught him in the record store, late one night after closing hours. Dave had a lamp on the counter by the cash. He had taken the shade off the lamp. He had the lamp on and was hovering over the lit bulb, his mouth wide open. Kenny looked at him and said, "It's moths that are attracted to light."

Dave said, "You're right. What are flies attracted to?"

Or the time in the drugstore when Dave got himself trapped in the blood pressure chair.

The cuff malfunctioned and began squeezing his arm. He panicked and sat there watching his blood pressure inch up. A crowd formed. His nose began to bleed. They called the fire department. They had to cut him out with the jaws of life.

"Are you telling me I can't go?" asked Dave.

"Of course not," said Morley. "Of course you should go. I'm just telling you not to do something stupid. I am telling you not to embarrass me. Or Marty."

Marty.

Dave's pal Marty from the early days. Of all the guys from back then—no one would have pegged *Marty* to be the guy to have a stroke. Two weeks ago. Standing in his living room.

"He is walking again," said Dave. "And they're talking about moving him to rehab. But he has to use one of those walkers, and Lillian says he is depressed. She says he doesn't seem to care. It's like he has given up. I have to go see him."

"I'm not saying you can't," said Morley. "I'm just saying I don't want any phone calls from the hospital."

And so Dave headed off on that most wistful of the small kindnesses. Headed off to visit a friend in hospital—a kindness that, in Dave's case, called for a certain degree of courage. Morley was right. Dave *didn't* do well in hospitals. In truth, hospitals terrify him.

Some people can walk into a hospital and be overcome by the milk of human kindness. Be struck by the way that we care for each other, the way we circle the wagons and do *our best* for those of us who aren't at *our best*.

All Dave sees is the cold clinical terror of the places. Each corridor, each direction sign, each little department a nagging reminder of everything that can go wrong with a human body.

It was a beautiful morning. He decided to walk. He stopped in at Lawlor's Drugs along the way and bought himself a bottle of hand sanitizer.

A person could be kind, but that didn't mean a person shouldn't be careful. He was, after all, about to expose himself to bugs that would wipe you out as soon as look at you.

Marty had a bed on the seventh floor. When Dave got there, he was lying in his bed looking pale and deflated. Like someone had let the air out of him. His eyes were shut and his mouth was open. He was drooling a little.

"Marty," said Dave. "You look great."

"I look terrible," said Marty. "You think they don't have mirrors here?"

They sat together for half an hour, not saying much. Sitting quietly, the way old friends sit when the only things to say are important things.

There was a box of tissues on the side table. Every ten minutes or so, Dave grabbed a tissue and wiped Marty's chin. He threw the tissues in the garbage pail in the bathroom. Every time he was in there, he pulled out his little bottle of sanitizer and rubbed some in his hands.

"I can smell that stuff," said Marty. "What? You think strokes are contagious?"

Dave had been there maybe an hour when the nurse showed up. When she walked in the room, he was lying in bed beside Marty. He had his sleeve rolled up and a blood pressure cuff wound around his upper arm.

"Oh," said Dave. "Hi."

He sat up, but he didn't look at her. His eyes didn't leave the silver line of mercury inching up the wall at the head of the bed. The line was moving. The nurse wasn't.

"This is mine," said Dave. He was pointing at the stethoscope around his neck. He had brought it with him in a plastic bag.

"I brought it with me" said Dave. "In case."

The nurse looked at Marty.

Marty said, "I have never seen him before in my life. He just walked in here and crawled into bed."

The nurse frowned. Marty had never cracked a joke before. She reached for her beeper.

Dave said, "Cripes, Marty."

Marty shrugged.

"It's okay," said Marty. "He's harmless."

Dave climbed out of the bed.

Dave looked at the nurse and said, "120 over 70. That's good, right?"

The nurse shook her head. She thought she'd seen everything.

She said, "We won't be long," and pulled a linen curtain around the bed and disappeared behind it.

Dave sat for a moment, then stood up and went outside. He found a lounge at the far end of the hall. No one else was there. He rested his forehead on the window. His breath fogged the glass and his view of the rooftops.

He stood like that for almost a minute. Then he jerked his head back, like he had received an electric shock. He pulled out his bottle of sanitizer and squeezed a little glob onto his fingers. He dabbed the stuff onto his lips, his forehead and the tip of his nose.

He was back in the room for maybe half an hour when he suggested they go outside.

"We should go for a walk," he said.

Marty rolled his eyes.

Dave said, "We could take a wheelchair. I could push you."

Marty said, "I'm not going out—like this."

Dave said, "It's beautiful out. It will make you feel better."

Marty said, "I'd feel like an idiot."

Dave looked at his friend, his sunken grey face, the blue hospital robe. Who would want to be seen looking like that?

He was going to argue. But he didn't argue. "Right," said Dave. He said it twice. "Right."

Then he said, "I will be right back. I won't be long."

He almost sprinted out of the room.

When he got back, Marty was asleep again, lying on his back, his mouth open, snoring quietly.

Dave reached out and put his hand on his shoulder.

"Hey," he said softly. "Hey."

Marty opened his eyes without moving. It took him a moment to register what he was looking at.

When he did, he shook his head. Back and forth. "No way."

Dave was standing beside the bed, beaming. He was wearing a light blue hospital gown. And nothing else.

Dave said, "One for all, all for one."

There was a wheelchair beside him.

He leaned over and grabbed Marty under the arms to help him out of the bed and into the chair.

Unfortunately, he hadn't put the brakes on the wheelchair. It wasn't the smoothest of transitions.

At one point Dave ended up sitting in the wheelchair with Marty in his lap—the chair rolling across the room. It looked like a nude, geriatric, go-carty sort of thing. But they finally did it.

"We did it," said Dave, panting.

As Dave pushed him down the corridor, Marty said, "Where did you get it?"

Dave said, "They have them in the lounge."

Marty said, "I mean the robe."

That's what had taken him so long. He had looked everywhere. Finally he had followed a porter onto an elevator. The porter was pushing a steel cart full of linen. As the porter gazed at the floor numbers chunking by, Dave grabbed the gown from the cart. He stuffed it under his jacket.

He changed in a washroom. On Marty's floor, at the far end of the hall.

"Where are your clothes?" asked Marty.

He had rolled his clothes up and hidden them on a shelf of supplies in the hallway. Swabs, masks, gowns, sterile pads. And Dave's clothes, stuffed at the back.

Marty and Dave took the elevator down to the main floor. The gowns they were both wearing were the ones that tied in the back. Dave's ended just above his knees. He looked ridiculous. Which, of course, was exactly the way he wanted to look.

They went out the back door into the little garden. They sat in the sun.

Marty said, "You're right. It is nice out here. Makes me feel— lighter."

Dave said, "How about going to Rebecca's for a coffee?"

Marty looked horrified. Marty said, "Are you crazy? I can't leave the hospital grounds. Some guy tried that last week. Some old guy. You should have seen what happened."

What had happened was they had called a *code yellow*. Missing patient.

Marty was twisting around in the wheelchair, trying to make eye contact with Dave.

"They shut down all the elevators. There were guards on all the doors.

"Times, times have changed, Dave. You can't fool around the way we used to."

Dave wasn't listening. Dave was pushing Marty towards the sidewalk. Dave believed the outing would do Marty good.

"Oh no," said Marty. "Here we go."

They were heading to a little café in Anderson Mill. A place Marty went all the time.

They got their coffees—two flat whites. They sat in a park by a school.

It was nearly four in the afternoon when Dave wheeled Marty back to his room.

Dave wasn't about to admit it, but he felt a sense of relief to be back. He had spotted a security guy watching them in front of the hospital. He had felt a rush of panic. He thought the guy was going to bust them. Dear God. He was determined not to mess this up.

Marty hadn't noticed.

Marty said, "That was good. The coffee. You were right. I enjoyed it."

Dave said, "We'll do it again."

"Thanks," said Marty. "I have been feeling …" He didn't want to say it. But he did. "Sad."

Neither of them moved for a moment. Then Dave leaned over and gave Marty a hug.

"I'll see you," he said.

As he left, he reached around to his backside, thinking to himself that when he was leaned over, hugging Marty, there'd been a full moonrise, no doubt about it.

He wandered down to the cart where he had hidden his clothes.

The cart was gone.

Dave looked at where the cart was supposed to be. He said, "Oh, come on."

There was a handicap bathroom down the hall. He went in and locked the door behind him. He needed a moment alone. He needed to figure this out. He stood in the darkness for a minute, staring at the locked door. Then he flicked on the lights and just about jumped out of his skin. There was someone in there with him.

"Excuse me!" he said, jumping. "I'm so sorry."

The stranger jumped at *exactly* the same moment he did. He said *exactly* the same thing.

Dave realized he was staring at his blue-robed self in the mirror.

He was just about to open the washroom door when he heard the announcement. *Code yellow. Code yellow. Code yellow.*

The woman on the public address system repeated herself three times. He stood there with his hand on the door, listening intently.

Were they talking about him and Marty? Had the security guard filed a report?

The PA system interrupted his questions. *Code yellow,* said the woman one more time. Then she said, *White, middle-aged patient. Brown hair.*

Could have been anyone. Which meant, of course, it could have been Dave.

Locked in the seventh floor bathroom, Dave frowned. This was not good news.

What did he know? Well, he knew this—he knew he had to get out of the hospital without a scene. And to do that, he had to get out without anyone seeing him. He opened the bathroom door and looked around the hallway.

There was a stairwell at the far end of the hall. He figured there would be a fire door at the bottom.

He figured right.

He made it all the way to the second floor before he heard the burst of radio static coming up the stairwell towards him.

He stopped and peered over the railing. He saw the security guard from outside.

How could he possibly explain himself? Sneaking down the stairwell in a hospital gown during a code yellow.

All he knew was he didn't want Morley getting a phone call from hospital security.

So he slipped through the exit door and out onto the second floor. And then, without stopping to think, into the first room he came upon.

A patient's room. And gloriously empty. He went into the bathroom and shut the door.

His heart was pounding. He waited for an eternity. Then he stood up and walked towards the door. The security guard was standing in the hallway waiting for him. Their eyes locked. Dave smiled. And in a moment of divine inspiration, he crossed the empty room and crawled back into the bed.

The guard came into the room and stared at him. Dave closed his eyes and pretended he was going to sleep.

The guard left.

While Dave lay there, trying to settle his heart and pondering his next move, a nurse breezed in carrying a dinner tray.

"Hello," she said. "My name is Dana. It's suppertime."

She placed a tray on the tall table by the bed and pushed it in front of him. Then she stood there. The only thing Dave could do was to eat the meal.

"It's good," said Dave, as he spooned the cold mashed potatoes into his mouth.

"Eat your dessert," said the nurse. She was pointing at the bowl of applesauce.

"Thanks," said Dave. "I'm okay."

The nurse smiled cheerfully.

"I mixed your medication into it," she said. "It will help you sleep."

And she picked up his spoon. Dave watched in horror as she dipped it into the drugged applesauce. She held the spoon up to his mouth.

"Open up," she said.

What else could he do?

She made sure he finished every last bit.

When he woke up, he was on a gurney. There was a man in blue scrubs wheeling him down a corridor.

"Hey," said the man in the scrubs. "You ready?"

"What?" said Dave. He tried to sit up.

But he couldn't sit up.

He was strapped to the gurney.

"What are these straps for?" he asked.

The man in the scrubs said, "People often lash out during the procedure."

"There's been a mistake." Dave said. "I don't need a procedure."

The orderly said, "That's what they all say."

The orderly manoeuvred the cart around a corner and into a room that looked exactly like the birthing room.

Except it wasn't the birthing room. Dave caught a sign on the door as it swung shut behind him.

Proctology.

By the book, the orderly should not have left Dave alone in there.

But he did.

It was only two minutes, and he was, after all, strapped down.

When he returned, Dave *was* still strapped to the gurney. But he was no longer lying on top of it.

He had flipped it over. The gurney was on top of him. He was trying to squirm his way to the door with the gurney tied on his back.

No hands.

He looked like a seal on an ice floe.

The next time he came to, he was in the emergency ward. A young intern was stitching up a gash in his head.

Marty was sitting in the corner. Marty was beaming.

Marty had heard the code yellow and put two and two together.

It was Marty who'd identified him.

"Hey," said Marty when Dave opened his eyes. "You look good."

"I look terrible," said Dave. Then he looked at the intern. "He told you I'm not the missing guy?"

"Oh yeah," said Marty. "That was some guy who was supposed to be having a proctology procedure."

Dave sat up and looked at the clock on the wall. It was after eight.

Dave said, "I'm so out of here."

The intern was shaking his head.

"Head injury," said Marty. "You're in for twenty-four hours' observation. They put you in my room."

An hour later they were lying in their respective beds. Dave tugging at the ID bracelet they had put on his wrist.

Marty was having the time of his life. Marty was holding up his cellphone, waving it back and forth.

"You've got to phone her sometime," said Marty.

Dave said, "You call for me. Tell her there was an accident. Tell her I'm in a coma."

Marty said, "I'm a stroke victim. That's too sophisticated for me."

He flipped the cellphone across the room. Dave caught it.

Marty sank back onto his pillows. He reached back and turned off the lights. The two of them lay there in the darkness for maybe five minutes. Then Marty giggled and smiled, and across the dark room he said, "Good night, John-Boy."

Marty hadn't had this much fun for years.

LE MORTE D'ARTHUR

There are serpents among us!
—PEARL McCOY

It was a summer evening—the heat of the day was done, but night was nowhere in sight. It was that lovely time *between* time. It was dusk. Everything was faded—as if the world had been stonewashed.

Dave was driving through the countryside—around the long corners, over the low hills.

"Corn's up nice," he said.

No one said anything in reply. No one had said anything for half an hour.

The silent ones were Stephanie, sitting in the front seat beside Dave but staring out the window, away from him, and Sam, sitting in the back.

Dave shrugged and fumbled with the button on the armrest of his door. His window slid down. He stuck his left arm out and let it ride on the current.

A convertible passed them going in the opposite direction. Dave said, "The problem with convertibles is there is only fifteen minutes a year when you would want to have the roof down. The rest of the time is either too hot or too cold."

Still not a word.

"I think this," said Dave, not giving up, "this moment, right now, is this year's fifteen minutes."

Still silence.

"Right now," said Dave, again.

Finally, Sam said, "When I get a car, it's going to be a convertible. And I am *always* going to have the roof down."

Dave said, "Yeah? What kind of convertible are you going to get?"

"I dunno," said Sam.

It got quiet again. Five minutes quiet. Ten …

Dave started to sing. "Twilight Time."

Louder than one should.

"Dad," said Stephanie, dragging it over two syllables.

Dave said, "That was a big hit for the Platters."

Stephanie let out a long sigh.

She said, "I don't care."

At least they were talking.

Then Stephanie said, "… I can't stop thinking about Arthur."

"Me too," said Dave. "Me too."

Arthur, the dog, was sick. They weren't sure how sick.

"Is he going to die?" asked Sam.

"We don't know," said Dave. "We don't know."

"If we don't *know*," said Stephanie, "why did you come and get me?"

Good question, thought Dave.

They had driven … what? Two-and-a-half hours that afternoon, Dave and Sam, to pick her up. They had eaten supper along the way, at a little place by the river. And now they were driving home—the three of them.

"I just thought you should see him," he said.

"So he *is* going to die," said Stephanie.

"We don't know that," said Dave.

But he was going to die. If not now, soon. They all knew that. That's why all the quiet. Arthur was old. And now he was old and sick.

They rolled along, quietly. Until a little while later when Dave said something under his breath.

"What?" said Sam.

Dave said, "Oh. I was just thinking of *my* old dog."

Sam asked, "How did *he* die?"

Dave said, "I wasn't there. I was away."

Scout. A mutt. Black and white coat, strong legs, built for running. There was probably some border collie in him: he had the loyalty and the focus, but not the brains. Definitely not the brains. Scout was one dumb dog.

"He was one dumb dog," said Dave.

This was back when Dave was a boy and living in Big Narrows. Back when people built their own homes. You'd start with the basement and live in the basement until you could afford to go higher. Scout, born in some basement, always stayed close to the ground. Scout *hated* water.

It drove Dave's dad, Charlie, a duck hunter, to distraction.

"A dog should know how to swim," he'd say every year as duck season approached.

One spring Charlie decided to do something about that. They drove to town. Charlie threw Scout off the government pier.

Scout sank like a stone. He didn't even try. He went straight down, until he reached a point of stasis about three feet below the surface, and he hovered there, looking up at them. Sorrowfully.

"Oh no," said Charlie, down on his knees, peering into the water, calling the dog.

Scout's mouth appeared to be opening and closing. It looked as if he was barking, underwater.

"Oh no," said Charlie again.

Dave and his sister, Annie, were both there, standing beside their dad, pointing and crying.

There was nothing for Charlie to do but yank off his jacket and jump in. This was Mother's Day weekend. Bras d'Or Lake in May. Not even the teenagers were thinking of swimming.

When Charlie hit the water, he gasped. He almost sank himself. When he told the story later, that's the part he would start with: "It was close, I'll tell you."

And that's just when he *hit* the water. He knew it was going to be colder *below* the surface.

But he couldn't let the dog drown, not with the kids standing there bawling their eyes out. Not with witnesses.

So Charlie sucked in a lungful of air, ducked under, grabbed Scout by the tail and swam him over to the beach.

"So, he saved him," said Sam.

The sun was pretty much gone now; night was settling around the car. The darkness that was obscuring the world was working them together. This was the way Dave had hoped it would be. The three of them, driving along, talking as they went.

He said, "Hand me the Thermos."

Stephanie opened the silver Thermos and poured milky tea into the black lid and held it out for him.

"Thanks," he said.

Then he said, "Scout was never taken on a walk in his life."

"What do you mean?" asked Sam.

"He used to walk *us*," said Dave.

When the weather was good, Scout walked to school with Dave and Annie. He would drop them off and then meet them at the end of the day.

"He was always waiting in the wings," said Dave. "I have no idea what he did in between."

There was plenty for him to do. Scout was a small-town dog. He had a full life. Mostly he hung out with the other dogs and barked. Mostly they did that back of Kerrigan's grocery store. On a good day, the butcher would slip someone a bone. And then there would be a fight to see who got it.

Sometimes one of them would slip *into* the store and grab meat right off the counter. Not Scout. But there were dogs in town who would do that. They were dogs, after all—they believed in invisibility. They figured if they were fast enough, even if they were seen, no one would recognize them.

"Did I ever tell you about the day he went to church?" asked Dave.

Stephanie rolled her eyes.

Dave wasn't fussed by that. He knew he had told them before. He knew what he was doing. You *have* to tell stories over and over. It is the creation of myth. The only road to immortality.

"Tell it," said Sam.

"Of all the things he did," said Dave, "this was probably the best."

By *the best* he meant *the worst*.

"It was summer," said Dave. "We were driving our mother crazy."

"Who?" said Sam.

"Me and Annie," said Dave. "Your aunt, Annie.

"So my mother decided that on Sundays, everyone was going to go to church. Except her. So she could have some time alone."

So Sunday mornings, they'd all set off. Charlie took his truck, but Dave and Annie walked. They followed the railway tracks into town, where they would pool their money and buy a pop or a box of potato chips, then head out of town over the bridge and up the hill to church.

"We would head out around nine for the eleven o'clock service," said Dave.

The Sunday he was telling them about, the famous Sunday, they got to town, and there was Scout in front of the Maple Leaf Restaurant. He had his nose in a french fry box. He was *covered* in ketchup.

The moment he spotted Dave and Annie, Scout decided he was going to go with them—wherever it was they were going. The church was in the same general direction as the trout pond, and you never knew—there could be fish heads involved.

Dave and Annie knew letting Scout follow them to church was not a good idea.

"So we stood there," said Dave, "and told Scout to go home."

"And did he go?" said Sam.

"Of course not," said Dave.

"He followed them," said Stephanie.

"But not on the road," said Dave. "In the woods, *paralleling* the road. He had been hanging around bad company. He figured we couldn't see him.

"When we got to the bridge," said Dave, "we stopped and called him: 'Come here, boy. Come on.'"

"And then what?" asked Sam.

"We threw stuff at him," said Dave. "Sand."

They made it up the church hill just in time—the church bell ringing, and no Scout in sight.

"Though I did have a bad feeling," said Dave.

Charlie was already there. They slipped into the pew beside him.

Now, Charlie went to church for the same reason they did— because Margaret told him to. He made no bones about it. He would cut articles out of the *Reader's Digest* and slip them in the hymnal and read for most of the service. He would look up occasionally and mutter unhelpful things like, "Father O'Neill is climbing new heights on Mount Monotony today."

"Anyway," said Dave. "The three of us were sitting right near the front."

When they heard a murmur from the back of church, Annie, who was on the aisle, turned around.

Annie said, "Don't look now."

"It was Scout," said Sam.

"That's right," said Dave. "But I couldn't see him."

Scout, who had finally arrived at church, had decided he would sneak up to the front to join Dave and Annie. So he had slid under the back pew and was worming his way forward row by row—invisibly. Or so he thought.

Sadly, on his way through the woods, Scout had managed to pick up a stick. The stick was attached to his undercarriage, dragging behind him. There were some other things attached to his belly—some coral-coloured muck that he had rolled in and was matted in his fur, and something horrible and foul smelling.

It was hot in the church that July afternoon and a heavy sense of torpor had settled on the congregation. Father O'Neill, who was about to begin his homily, sensed he was losing everyone. He had been watching Valentine Kavanagh. Valentine had been fighting off sleep for a good ten minutes—his head drifting towards his chest and then snapping back as if he had been shot. But he had finally given in. Valentine's head was hanging lifelessly from his neck. He was snoring softly.

Father O'Neill was just coming to the part where the Israelites are punished for speaking out against God and Moses.

In an attempt to raise Valentine from his siesta, and to get the attention of everyone else, Father O'Neill slammed his hand down on the pulpit and bellowed, "The Lord sent fiery serpents among the people and they bit the people and many died!"

And that is when Scout popped up under Valentine's pew and nuzzled old Valentine's hand with his ketchup-covered snout. Valentine, who had been dreaming about biting serpents, blinked one eye open. And there was Scout grinning up at him.

He had no doubt that Scout was a serpent. When Scout licked his hand, Valentine lurched out of his seat and screamed, "Jesus save me!"

Scout dove under the next pew, and came up between Lillian McAllister's outstretched legs. She saw him and fainted. It was Pearl McCoy who stood up and called out, "There are serpents among us."

Father O'Neill leaned forward to see the serpents for himself. He knocked the pulpit over.

As it went down, he caught a glimpse of Scout and said, "Dear God, serpents," and that was more or less the end of the service.

"Scout came right up to us," said Dave. "His tail wagging, as if to say, 'Isn't church great?'"

"But how did he die?" asked Sam.

"Oh," said Dave.

And now it was his turn to be silent.

"I was away," he said finally. "He was hit by a car."

"And he was killed," said Sam.

"No," said Dave. "He made it home. He died a couple of days later. I have always felt bad that I didn't go home and, you know, see him."

"Why didn't you?" asked Stephanie.

"I was working, and I figured if he made it home, he was going to be all right."

Then he said, "No one said I should. Go home, I mean."

Fifteen minutes later, Dave pulled into a general store in the middle of nowhere—the only store on a country corner. They parked beside a phone booth, under the yellow glow of a street lamp. They got Popsicles and a bag of chips.

While they were walking back to the car, Dave looked at his daughter. "You want to drive?"

She shook her head.

When they got back on the highway, they were quiet again, but it was a different kind of quiet, a together sort of quiet, not an apart one.

Sam said, "Tell the one about Arthur and the potatoes."

"There's not much to tell," said Dave.

"Just tell it," said Sam.

"He used to sit on potatoes," said Dave.

"Like he was trying to hatch them," said Sam.

"If we wanted to cook potatoes, we had to pull them out from under him," said Dave.

Stephanie said, "That is so gross."

"And sleeping on the vent," said Sam.

"In our bedroom," said Dave. "Mom and I froze one whole winter. Because he was sucking up all the heat."

"And you couldn't figure it out," said Sam.

"We brought the furnace guy in," said Dave.

"Twice," said Sam. "It was me who figured it out."

"That's right," said Dave.

"And the ice cream," said Sam.

"He was crazy for ice cream," said Dave.

"*Is*," said Stephanie. "He *is* crazy for ice cream."

It was after ten when they got to town. They drove by the vet's, but the vet was closed. So they went home. Morley was in the kitchen. When she saw Stephanie, she smiled, but only for a second. She smiled, and Stephanie smiled, and then one of them started to cry, and pretty soon, they were all crying.

"The vet called," said Morley. "He didn't make it. He went to sleep and didn't wake up."

And they stood there, the four of them in the kitchen. Arthur's empty basket by the back door.

We do this thing. We open our hearts to the world around us. And the more we do that, the more we allow ourselves to love, the more we are bound to find ourselves one day—like Dave, and Morley, and Sam, and Stephanie—standing in the kitchen of our life, surrounded by the ones we love, and feeling empty, and alone, and sad, and lost for words, because one of our loved ones, who should be there, is missing. Mother or father, brother or sister, wife or husband, or a dog or cat. It doesn't really matter. After a while, each death feels like all the deaths, and you stand there like everyone else has stood there before you, while the big wind of sadness blows around and through you.

"He was a great dog," said Dave.

"Yes," said Morley. "He was a great dog."

When he was a puppy, Arthur was allowed to sleep on Dave and Morley's bed. When he got bigger, they tried to move him onto the floor and found they had a battle on their hands. No dog in the world was as determined, or skilled, at insinuating himself onto a bed as Arthur.

They bought him a basket and put it in the hall just outside the bedroom door. Arthur would make a big deal of climbing into his basket every night—circling it neurotically, sighing and grunting as he worried his blanket into a pleasing hump. But as soon as Dave and Morley were breathing rhythmically, Arthur's head would rise like a periscope, and he would slide over the edge of his basket and work his way into the bedroom, keeping low to the ground—as if he were hunting. He would stop a foot short of the bed and cock an ear. If he didn't like the way one of them was breathing, he would bring his face close to theirs and listen, sometimes for five or ten minutes, staring at them like a priest taking confession, his wet nose only inches away from their faces.

One night Dave woke up when Arthur was in the middle of a reconnaissance. When he opened his eyes, all he could see were two huge eyeballs glaring back at him. Dave had no idea these were Arthur's eyeballs he was looking into. Then Arthur exhaled. Dave was enveloped by the sour smell of his dog's breath. It was like the breath of death, and he jerked upright. He woke Morley with his gasp. Arthur bounded back to his basket.

When Morley opened her eyes, Dave was pointing at the bedroom door.

"A serpent," he said.

Arthur was in his basket snoring. Pretending to snore.

If, however, when he crept into their bedroom, Arthur was satisfied that Dave and Morley were sound asleep, he would lift one paw slowly onto the bed and place it there without moving another muscle. If neither of them stirred, the other paw would go up just as slowly. Then rising, like a mummy rising from a crypt, Arthur would pull his body onto the bed and settle near their feet with a sigh, taking, at first, as little space as possible, but slowly unfolding, expanding as the night wore on—as if he were being inflated. He liked to work his body between theirs on his way towards the pillows.

"He stole my heart," said Dave. "Over and over. I'm so glad we had him with us."

"Have," said Sam. "*Have* him with us."

And Sam got up and went to the cupboard and got a potato, and without a word walked over and dropped it into Arthur's basket.

"He's still here," he said. "He always will be."